Conch Republic

Vol. III
Coba Libre

Look for other Western & Adventure novels
by
Eric H. Heisner

Along to Presidio

West to Bravo

Seven Fingers a' Brazos

Above the Llano

T. H. Elkman

Mexico Sky

Short Western Tales: Friend of the Devil

Wings of the Pirate

Africa Tusk

Fire Angels

Cicada

Citation for Murder

Conch Republic, Island Stepping with Hemingway

Conch Republic – vol. 2, Errol Flynn's Treasure

Follow book releases and film productions at:
www.leandogproductions.com

Conch Republic
Vol. III
Coba Libre

Eric H. Heisner

Illustrations by Emily Jean Mitchell

Visit our website at
www.leandogproductions.com

Illustrations by: Emily Jean Mitchell
Contact: mlemitche@gmail.com
Website: www.mlemitchellart.com

Dustcover jacket design: Dreamscape Cover Designs

Underwater diving photo by: Sae Cho

Edited by: Story Perfect Editing Services – Tim Haughian

Paperback ISBN: 978-1-956417-09-8

Printed in the United States of America

Dedication

To adventures lived, not just observed.

Special Thanks

Libby Thomas Bentley, Amber Word Heisner,
Emily Jean Mitchell, & Sae Cho

Note from Author

Some folks think it takes a lot of money to travel. Sure, it can make the trip a lot easier, but the lack of funds should never be an excuse to pass up an opportunity for enrichment. As I mentioned in the first volume of *Conch Republic*, I lived in my truck for an extended period in the Florida Keys – I sure wasn't rich! When I was twenty, I had the opportunity to backpack around Europe with three girls for two months. Sleeping on trains, living on a fifty-dollars-a-day budget, and coming home with less than a hundred bucks left to my name… I definitely wasn't rich.

These are the things that develop character. I have a good friend who works a whole lot, owning his own business. When the mention of a trip comes up, he is the first to say, "Let's do it – Good Times!". I have been on adventures with him in Costa Rica, El Salvador, and of course the Florida Keys. I have another friend that travels all over the world wearing a fancy dress she had to buy to be a bridesmaid in a wedding. No matter the travel companion, wanderlust opens your eyes to the world and the many sorts of people who live in it.

My fortune cookie says, "No matter your comfort… Travel, and you will be rewarded many times over."

Eric H. Heisner

April 23, 2023

I

Just beyond the open hangar doors of Key West Air Charters, a shiny, black limousine is waiting. The morning sun lights up the eastern horizon and puts a glow to the cloud of exhaust that comes from the tailpipe of the elongated luxury vehicle. Beyond the parked car, above the sea ramp, the seaplane with its high wing and large radial engines sits with its nose pointed out to the gently rolling waters surrounding Stock Island.

The tap of men's leather-soled dress shoes sounds off the concrete floor inside the hangar. A businessman in a high-priced suit exits, followed by Rollie in his rumpled pilot attire. When the driver's door of the limo clicks open, a chauffeur gets out and goes around to stand at the rear passenger-side door. Stopping outside the hangar doors, the businessman extends a hand to Rollie, and they confirm a deal with a shake.

1

Eric H. Heisner

Rollie stands watching, as the man gets inside the car. The driver shuts the door, steps around and gets back inside. With a rev of the vehicle's V8 engine, the limo drives backward, swings around and goes out through the front gate entrance. With the early morning sun cresting the horizon and shining on his face, Rollie gives a wave and heads back inside.

Stepping into the sectioned-off office inside the hangar, Rollie momentarily glances over his shoulder before closing the door behind him. He turns to the partner desk in the middle of the room and grabs a fat envelope from the top of the cluttered mess. Peeking inside, Rollie thumbs through a thick stack of one-hundred-dollar bills.

Satisfied with the amount, Rollie moves across the room to a framed picture on the wall of a China Clipper coming in for a water landing on a South Pacific Island cove. He swings the artwork outward on its hidden hinge to reveal a wall safe. Rollie spins the numbered dial to enter the combination and pulls open the fireproof door. He takes out several crisp bills and tosses the envelope with the remainder into the safe.

Rollie swings the metal door shut, latches the handle and gives the dial a good spin. He conceals the vault again with the framed seaplane art and then grabs an empty duffle from the top of a filing cabinet. Tossing the canvas bag on top of the desk, he goes around to his side, scoots his chair back, and pulls open the top drawer. After taking out an American passport and putting it in the bag, he then pulls out a handgun.

Coba Libre

Through the dirty, office windows, Rollie looks to the mechanic shop. His gaze then travels to the open hangar doors. He stares at the WWII vintage plane parked above the ramp. After a moment of considering the details of the upcoming job, Rollie reaches back into the desk, takes out a box of cartridges, and tucks them inside the duffle bag alongside the handgun. Finally, Rollie slips a few bills of cash into his passport and folds the remainder into his pocket.

~*~

Secluded in a small apartment above a carriage house, the writer Jonathan T. Springer spends the early part of his day at a desk, clicking away on a laptop keyboard. His writing pace is steady and deliberate, lost in the world of his creative thoughts. As the morning sunlight peeks through the slatted plantation shutters, Jon pauses and then clicks several more keys to type *The End*.

Pushing back in his chair, Jon looks over at a bottle of Blackwell rum sitting beside a hand-rolled cigar resting on the rim of a cocktail glass. He puts the Cuban cigar in his mouth, grabs the dark bottle and pours himself two fingers of rum. With the thick cigar clenched in his teeth, Jon lifts the glass, swirls the amber liquor inside and takes a sniff.

Suddenly, the telephone rings. Glancing to see that the clock on the computer reads 6:58 AM, he swivels his chair and reaches over to the old-fashioned rotary phone. Snatching the handset from the cradle, Jon answers. "Hello…?"

"Hey there, Johnny-boy!"

Jon glances to the clock again and does the calculation of time zone difference from Key West to Los Angeles. "Moselly, what are you doing up at this hour?"

"Hey pal, the loyal and trustworthy agent never rests, until he has done everything he can for his star client."

"Is that so?"

"You bet, buddy-boy!"

Jon takes the cigar from his mouth and licks his lips. "Are you drunk?"

"Yeppers, but I have one of those new self-driving cars, so I should be fine as long as I put in the directions to the correct girlfriend. One time, I was talking to one lady on the phone, and it took me to the apartment of the other one... Hot-damn, things got messy."

While sniffing his glass of rum, Jon looks at the clock. "Moselly, what's the call for?"

"Glad you asked. You see, I was at this very exclusive Hollywood party tonight. They were all talking about money, and I thought of you and that new book you're working on. How's it going? Can I see pages yet?"

Jon puts the cigar back between his teeth and answers. "Just finished it."

"What's that? You broke up there. Must be a bad phone connection to that secret island-hideaway you're staying in."

Taking the cigar from his mouth, Jon repeats himself. "Moselly, I just finished the manuscript."

"What... Really!? Why haven't I received it yet?"

"Because, I just finished it."

"Heck! What are you waiting for? Send it over."

Swirling his drink a few times, Jon shakes his head. "Thought I might go through it once more for good measure." He puts the cigar back in his mouth, closes his lips around it and opens a matchbox from *Conch Republic Tavern*.

"Fine, fine, fine... You do that, but send it to me first so I can have a look. My star client runs off to the Caribbean and hasn't delivered any pages in months, and now he's being coy. Send it now, if not sooner."

"Shouldn't you be in bed?"

"Yes, but I'm not sure where this car is taking me."

"Bye, Moselly."

"Send me those pages!" The call disconnects, and Jon hangs up the receiver.

A beam of sunlight catches Jon's attention, and he turns to the window. He looks at the computer clock again – 7:01 AM. He takes another sniff of the rum in his glass and takes the cigar out of his mouth. Licking his lips, he mutters to himself. "Damn... If I had finished just a bit earlier, it still would've felt like yesterday."

He puts the glass and unlit cigar aside, clicks *Save* on the finished manuscript and folds the screen down on the laptop. He leans back in his chair, looks to the celebratory drink and smoke, and then stretches his arms up high over his head. "Well, I guess I'll go for a run instead."

II

While municipal street sweepers rumble and leaf blowers howl, feral chickens run wild on the island streets of Key West. Water splashes over the curb, as a Duval Street business-owner sprays a hose at a stain on the sidewalk. Outfitted in a t-shirt, shorts and running shoes, Jon jumps the stream of water and continues his jog.

He trots past the high brick wall surrounding Hemingway's house, down to the Southernmost Point mile marker and hooks a left, heading toward Smathers Beach. Feeling the invigorating rush of having just completed what he considers his first serious work of novel writing, Jon runs with the wind blowing his hair and his feet light on the pavement. After a hard sprint along the beach, he cuts north up First Street, past the High School, and angles toward the city cemetery.

Eric H. Heisner

As he approaches the wrought iron fence, Jon slows to a walk and catches his breath. He looks inside at the grave markers and monuments, and then he stops to read the sign near the entrance. While using his shirt sleeve to wipe sweat from his face, Jon discovers that the graveyard was moved to the highest point on the island after a hurricane destroyed the old cemetery in 1847. He wanders inside and walks between the headstones. Stopping before an oversized memorial shaped like a conch shell put on end, Jon reads the marker:

Sir Peter Anderson, Secretary General of the Conch Republic, January 12, 1947 – July 16, 2014 "HE HAD FUN"

Pondering his newly chosen island lifestyle, literary focus, and the unique grave marker, Jon looks up at the wide, pink opening in the conch shell. He leans forward to peer into the void and unexpectedly a familiar voice echoes from inside. "Hey dere, writer-mon. You lookin' fer someone?"

Momentarily shaken, Jon wipes the sweat from his eyes. He sighs with relief, when he sees the island sage, Aston, step out from behind the large conch shell. The scruffy islander, with a parrot perched on his shoulder, cracks a wide grin as Jon greets him. "Hey there, Aston. Was just on a run and got curious about this place as I passed by."

"Dis is da place of island history. If you curious 'bout da past or future, dere is many a hint to guide yer way in an old cemetery." Aston strokes the feathers of his bird and steps around to stand next to Jon. He smiles fondly at the grave marker. "He sure did have fun."

"Yeah? More than most?"

The islander chuckles. "Yes, I do believe it was more dan most would want to have." Aston waves his hand as he walks away, calling over his free shoulder, "Come along, writer-mon. Dis is one you might like to see…"

Following Aston, Jon wipes his face on his sleeve again and walks further into the burial grounds. He walks past specific sections and grave markers that reflect the cultural diversity of the Keys. From Jewish to Catholic, including black, white and islander, and veterans of the Civil War from both the North and the South. Aston stops before a grave site that is decorated with opened beer cans, half-smoked cigars and a smattering of tossed coins. Beneath an arrangement of dirty plastic flowers, the inscription reads:

Joseph S. Russell, December 9, 1889 – June 20, 1941
THO LOST TO SIGHT, TO MEMORY DEAR

Jon stares at the grave marker and the odd tributes. "Who is this person?"

Aston takes a knee and sweeps away a few blades of cut grass, leaving the coins and cigars in place. "Dis here man was da most famous barkeep of da Keys as well as a fishing guide and rumrunner."

Amazed, Jon utters, "Joe Russell? The boat captain and run-around pal of Ernest Hemingway…?"

"Dis where his road of adventure come to an end."

Staring at the inscription, Jon comments, "He died on June 20, Errol Flynn's thirty-second birthday."

Setting his bird on the ground to stretch its legs, Aston stands closer to Jon and whispers, "Dar is many a people who die and were born on da same date. It is what you do b'tween birth 'n death days dat makes folks remember you."

Jon gazes around the cemetery at all the untold stories. He has a sudden pang of creative energy and feels the urge to get back to his writing. "This place is inspiring."

Aston nods. "And, *mostly* quiet..." The islander gives a broad wink and adds, "Usually." He scoops up his bird, places it on his shoulder and gives a wave goodbye as he walks off. "See ya 'round 'gain sometime, writer-mon. Do some good." Jon watches him speak quietly to his bird, turn behind an aged stone mausoleum and then disappear from sight.

A short while later he can hear the grinding clank of Aston's bike chain, as the decorated beach cruiser rattles down the street. He watches for them a moment, and then catches a glimpse of the quirky islander and flapping parrot wings as they ride away. Damp with sweat, Jon looks to the morning sun as he exits the graveyard. He breathes in the warm humidity of the Caribbean and trots off.

III

Seated at his writing table, Jon clicks steadily at the keyboard. He stops, looks to the flashing cursor on the screen and then types a few words to edit his recent work. The phone rings, breaking him from his concentration. He reaches over and lifts the receiver from the cradle. "Hello?"

A woman's voice comes on the line. "Good morning... Hello, is this Jonathan T. Springer?"

"Yes, and who is this?"

"I work at the reception desk for C. Moselly Literary Agency in Los Angeles."

"Okay?"

"I have a message for you."

"Go ahead."

"Mister Moselly is requesting the recent manuscript you promised him."

"I'll send it when it's ready."

After a pause, the woman continues, "He would like to know when to expect it."

"Tell him it should arrive at his desk on island time." There is silence on the phone, much longer this time, until the receptionist finally responds. "Yes, okay... On island time. What time would that be exactly?"

"When I send it..."

"Oh, okay... I will tell him you will send it asap."

"You can tell him whatever you'd like." John can hear her scribbling down notes on paper before she speaks again. "There is one other item here on the call form."

"Yes, what is it?"

"He would like to know when you plan to get your cell phone returned, or if there is a new contact number?"

"I don't have a cell phone anymore."

"It says here that we are currently paying the bill for one, and when the certain phone number is called there is, I quote – *A long-winded lady from the Midwest who answers*."

Becoming annoyed with the call, Jon answers deadpan. "I don't know what to tell you."

"Should we issue a new phone number and send a replacement mobile telephone to your current address?"

"No."

"What about the phone bill?"

"Don't send that either."

"No... What do we *do* about it?"

"I'd stop paying it."

The receptionist scribbles another note and utters, "Okay. I will pass along your message."

"I didn't give you a message."

"We will expect the pages for review shortly."

"It's good to have expectations." Jon turns in his chair to have a look out the window.

"Yes… Have a nice day…"

"You too…" He hangs up the phone, looks at the thin white cord connected to the wall and briefly considers unplugging it. Turning back to his laptop computer, he stares at the screen, sighs at the loss of his train of thought and clicks the *Save* icon. He folds the screen down, pushes back in his chair and glances out the windows again. "I wonder who is over at the Conch Republic Tavern today…"

Jon pulls off his t-shirt and tosses it into the bathroom. He grabs a casual button-down that is draped over the back of a chair and puts it on. After slipping on some leather sandals, he heads out the door.

~*~

The thoroughfare through Old Town is full of activity, but not with the exceedingly busy crowd of tourists that happens when a cruise ship unloads. Jon carelessly strolls, glancing into shop windows and weaving around clusters of people congregating on the sidewalk. He turns at the corner, walks down a block, and ducks into the garden entrance leading to the Conch Republic Tavern.

Jon enters the old-fashioned pub and goes to the bar. Before he can lift a leg over an empty stool, an attractive woman behind the bar ambles over, tosses out a drink coaster, and sets a pint of Sunset Ale in front of him. He smiles at the bartender and touches the chilled beer glass. "Wow, Angie… Did you have this poured before I walked in the door?"

Angie Storm, the bar's owner, glances at her empty wrist as if there was a timepiece there and flashes a smile. "You're not a lot of things, but being predictable is something you are, my writing friend."

"Well, quality is better than quantity I guess?"

"In this business, it's good to have a mix of both."

Seated at the other end of the bar, Ace, the mechanic from Key West Air Charters looks over and calls out to them. "Hey now, I resemble that remark!"

Jon turns toward Ace, lifts his beer glass with a saluting gesture and takes a drink. "How ya doin' Ace?"

"It's my day off, so I'm doin' jest fine."

Jon thinks a second, then looks across the bar at Angie. "What day is it?"

"Tuesday."

Jon consents with a nod. "I usually take Sundays off, so I can keep track of the week."

Ace takes a swig from his beer and shrugs. "I take any day off that suits me."

Turning to lean back on the bar top, Jon asks, "How do you keep track of the day of the week?"

"Hey, I do what I love every day, and I'm lucky to work with good people. What's there to keep track of?"

Coba Libre

Jon takes another drink and ponders the thought. "Yeah, I guess I'm adjusting to the rhythm of island time."

Angie taps her fingers on the bar and then starts to go and serve another customer. "Don't go changing your clock... Or, you'll be as uninteresting as the rest of us."

Jon watches her stroll away and can't help but admire her athletic figure. Taking his beer along, Jon moves down the bar to occupy a stool next to Ace. "What's Rollie up to...?"

"Well, he might be out of my hair for almost a week. Told me this morning that he chartered a gig with a business fella headed to the Yucatan Peninsula." Ace cracks a sly grin. "He even paid me a bonus."

"A bonus...? That's nice!"

"Yeah, I like to call 'em *Bigfoot bonuses*."

"Why?"

"You hear about 'em a lot, but never see 'em."

"He's going to Mexico?"

"Yeah, dropping a client off and then taking some time to explore the Quintana Roo coast, down to Belize."

Jon nods and takes another sip from his mug. "The pilot life is really a never-ending adventure for Rollie."

The mechanic shrugs. "When you have to clean up after 'im, it takes some of the charm out of it."

They both take a sip from their drinks and stare ahead. Occupying the pause in conversation, they glance down the bar at Angie working. She looks over at them, sees that they don't need another round of drinks yet and smiles at them. Adjusting his cap, Ace smooths his greying hair back and grins at Jon. "Life here ain't so bad either…"

IV

Daylight from the entryway of the tavern streams into the room catching everyone's attention. Jon and Ace both turn to look at the open door as Rollie steps in. The door swings shut, and the pilot lets his eyes adjust to the dimness of the room. Seeing the pair at the end of the bar, he heads toward them. "Hello, guys! What's doin'?"

Ace apprehensively looks to his nearly full beer glass and then back at the pilot. Jon pivots on his stool and smiles. "Nothing much... Just catching up."

Rollie waves down the bar to Angie and orders a drink. She confirms with a gesture, and he turns to Ace then Jon. "How's the writing, and where's that pretty blond of yours?"

Jon turns back around and sets his beer glass on the bar. "She had to get back home and go back to work."

"I figured she would be moving here to join you."

"No, she has a career to get back to in San Diego."

They watch as Angie brings Rollie a fresh beer and hands it across the bar. The pilot smiles at Jon and gives him a consoling pat on the back. "Didn't set the hook, eh?"

"Sometimes the story is all you come home with."

Overhearing the two men, Angie's curiosity is aroused. "You two go fishing recently?"

Rollie gives her a wink. "Jon here is more of a catch and release man." He looks at Jon. "Here's to the ones that got away." Lifting his glass, he takes a drink.

Angie looks at them strangely. "Are you talking fish?"

Jon replies, "I'm not much of an angler."

When she ultimately realizes they are talking about catching women instead of fishing, she rolls her eyes at him. "Thought you looked down. No Lizzy? Did she go home?"

"Yeah, she had work to get back to."

The bartender leans forward on the bar and tilts her head to Jon. "These islands aren't for everyone. Some folks get the feeling of coming home down here. Others stay a bit and then feel like going home."

Jon shakes his head. "It wasn't the location that deterred her from staying…"

Ace takes a gulp of beer and coughs under his breath. "Could it have been the crowd you were hanging with?"

Gazing to the bar back and the lineup of liquor bottles, Jon continues. "She explained that she didn't want to be a casualty of my mid-life crisis."

With a slight nod, Angie gives an expression of understanding. Rollie lifts his beer glass and mutters, "Huh… Is that what you're doing down here?"

"I didn't think so, but the way she put it made sense…" He takes another drink. "I didn't have much of an argument."

Noticing that the topic is making Jon uncomfortable, Angie turns the attention to Rollie and changes the subject. "Ace tells me you're headed to the coast of Mexico with some big-shot private charter?"

Cradling his drink, Rollie suddenly remembers his reason for coming in. "Oh yeah, that reminds me…"

Heaving a sigh, Ace droops his shoulders and gazes at his beverage which he thinks he might have to abandon. "Damn, I thought you'd never get around to asking."

Rollie acts surprised. "What do you mean?"

"Go ahead… Ask me."

Rollie looks around at the others and reluctantly sputters out, "Well… I wouldn't normally ask on your day off, but Sandy changed the oil and said I should talk to you."

Ace swipes his finger along the side of his cold glass. "What is it?"

Rollie shrugs. "That right engine is acting up."

Coba Libre

"You mean the left one?"

"I'm pretty sure it was the right."

Ace lowers his gaze and scoots his cold beer away. Begrudgingly, he slides off his stool and glances one more time at his unfinished beverage. "I'll take a look at it."

"Ace, I hate to ask for this favor, but we have that big client coming in tomorrow."

"I know."

"This one charter will keep us afloat for months."

Angie coughs, clearing her throat. "Maybe even settle an outstanding bar tab?"

Rollie pretends not to hear her and nudges Jon's arm. "How's your book coming? Want to go for a ride to Mexico?"

Jon glances at Ace who is staring at his unfinished beer. He pivots on his stool to turn back to Rollie and Angie. "Actually, I just finished up the manuscript I was working on, but I have to read it over again before it goes to my agent."

Impressed, Rollie nods. "Nothing like a little adventure to clear your mind."

Angie laughs while Jon gapes and retorts, "I haven't had a *little* adventure since I've been here."

Innocently, the pilot looks around the crowded tavern. "Yeah, but I'm the one who's always there to save your bacon. Would be great to have you flying right-seat for company."

Jon thinks on it, "What about the important client? Won't he mind?"

Rollie lifts his drink and takes a swallow. "Naw, he's not the type who would want to sit up in front. Too busy tapping on his phone. Checking the market, I guess."

"I don't know…"

"Come on… It will be an easy-going, fun time. Just a quick hop over to Cancun, drop the guy off, clear customs… We'll take a short cruise down the coast and meet up with some friends of mine in Tulum before heading back."

Jon considers the trip but wavers. "I really need to get some editing done."

"When is the deadline?"

Thinking a second, Jon realizes he doesn't have one. "Whenever I get it finished."

"Now you're sounding like a true Key West Islander. Heck, bring your laptop along, and you can do your edits on the white sandy beaches outside Julio's Hacienda."

"Who's hacienda?"

"Julio is an old flying pal of mine. He owns a place right on the beach now and guides tourists on local trips."

Hearing Julio's name, Ace heads for the door and grumbles, "Keep that crazy Mexican away from my plane…"

Rollie calls after him. "What was that, Ace?"

"You heard me."

Ace swings the door open, as Rollie hollers after him. "Tomorrow, take a few days off and enjoy a drink on me…" The door slams shut, and Rollie winces. "He's not happy."

Letting his eyes adjust after peering outside, Jon asks, "Suppose he's mad about the engine?"

"He doesn't mind that. It's Julio that he doesn't like." Angie moves away from them to serve other customers.

Jon turns to Rollie. "Why doesn't he like Julio?"

"Ace is funny that way… He'll give you the shirt off his back, but if you don't heed his advice and abuse an airplane, he'll never forgive you for it."

Curiosity piqued, Jon asks, "What happened?"

"We were working at an airstrip in Central America…"

Rollie takes a drink and looks over toward Angie. Making a gesture, he grabs her attention. Jon stares at him, waiting to hear more of the story. "And…?"

"Huh?"

"What did Julio do to piss-off Ace?"

Rollie turns back to Jon and smiles. "How about you hear it from the source? Come with me to Mexico, and Julio will tell you all kinds of legends and lies. There might even be a new book idea in it."

Jon shakes his head. "I don't know."

"It's a free trip for you, but I'm not gonna twist your arm. Wheels up at ten o'clock Wednesday morning."

Coming over again, Angie wipes down the bar top. "What's up, Rollie?"

"I need one of your deluxe care packages brought over to the hangar for my trip tomorrow."

"For how many?"

"It's for one guy and a valet, but he's a spender."

Angie smiles. "Yeah, unlike someone else I know."

Rollie gives her a sly look and pulls out a wad of cash from his pants pocket. He peels off a few large bills and slaps them on the bar. "Make it a special one with the high-end stuff. Ice, garnish, mixers and all the trimmings."

Angie seems more surprised at Rollie actually paying than at the dollar amount. She glances at Jon and swipes the bills off the bar. "Are you going along?"

"I haven't decided yet."

"Doesn't look like too bad a trip. I'll tuck a few bottles of Sunset ale in there for you." She turns to look at Rollie again. "Hey, why wasn't I invited on this one?"

Rollie grins wide and gives her a flirty blink of his eyes. "You got a new bikini to show off?"

She puts her hands behind her head in a sexy pose and replies, "On the beaches in Mexico, I go *sin ropa*."

The pilot gulps audibly and is speechless. Jon stares at them and asks, "What's *sin ropa*?"

"I'll tell you later." Rollie turns and heads to the door. "Thanks for sending over the traveling bar supplies, Angie." Daylight bursts into the barroom, and the pilot steps outside.

Jon looks at Angie, who laughs and grins mischievously, and he asks, "What hit him?"

She shrugs and flips the bar towel over her shoulder. "What's to keep you from the trip?"

Coba Libre

"My book, I guess."

"The one you've been working on for a while?"

"Yeah."

"What's the difference if it takes a little while longer? No deadline to keep, no commitments or expectations on you... Life is out there just waiting."

Jon takes a sip of beer and considers his unique status. "The way you say it, my life sounds pretty good."

"It is if you want it to be."

V

Afternoon sunlight filters through the trees overhanging the garage apartment. Near the window, Jon sits at his computer and reads over his manuscript. He pushes back in his chair, rests his eyes and then leans forward again.

The ringing telephone jolts him from his concentration. Annoyed, Jon looks at the vintage phone. He lifts the receiver, clicks the tabs on the cradle to disconnect the call and leaves the handset off the hook. "Stop calling me…"

He turns back to his work but has lost his desire to edit. Clicking on a tab to bring up the internet, Jon stares at a photo-filled page with a colorful tourist map of the Yucatan Peninsula. He calculates the distance to fly over the gulf from Key West to Mexico's thumb and murmurs to himself, "That's not all that far. He said it would be a quick trip."

Coba Libre

Jon's gaze travels to the corner of the room where his backpack sits, still packed from the last adventure to Jamaica. He leans back, looks at the palm trees outside the window and sighs, "All work and no play makes Jack a dull boy…"

~*~

The morning sun shines in Jon's face, as he walks, with the backpack slung on his shoulder, east toward Stock Island. He enjoys the tropical scenery, and the dampness of the early hour makes for a pleasant walk. After a peek at his wristwatch, Jon grimaces with concern and picks up the pace a bit.

At the rattling crank of a bicycle approaching from behind Jon turns to see Aston with his pet parrot, wings spread, careening toward him. He steps back from the curb, and watches as the pair come in for a landing.

"Hey dere, writer-mon!"

"Good morning, Aston."

"You's goin' to be late."

"For what?"

"Da Rollie-mon says dat you be commin' along to da Quintana Roo wit him today."

"I was considering it."

Aston scoots forward and pats the seat behind him. "Hop aboard! I git you dere 'n time." Jon eyes the elaborately decorated cruiser bike with banana seat and shakes his head. He starts on his way again. "No thanks… I can walk." Straddling the bicycle, Aston scoots his foot along the curb. "Yes, but you to be late, 'n have to walk back again."

Jon looks at the time on his wristwatch and back at the bike. "You want me to hop on behind and ride there with you?"

"Unless you have yer own ride, dis is da way to go." Aston pushes off, raises his feet and glides a bit while the bird squawks and flaps its wings.

"Looks dangerous…"

"Da most fun t'ings in life are sometimes dangerous."

Looking at his watch one more time, Jon pauses to think. "I can make it inside of forty minutes."

Aston flashes a big grin. "I kin get you dere in twenty."

Jon hangs his head, considers, and finally nods in favor. "Okay. Slide up more, so we don't give folks the wrong idea."

Aston laughs and perches on the front of the long seat. "Who knows what crazy, wild ideas dey have 'bout you or me?"

Jon stretches a leg over and places his feet up on the conch shell foot pegs. He holds onto the sissy bar behind and leans back so he doesn't get smacked in the face with the parrot's flapping wings. "Okay, driver-mon, ride on…"

Peering back at his reluctant passenger, Aston pushes off from the curb and chuckles. "Da last passenger I had on da back dere was yer pretty-blondie, special lady-friend."

"What?"

"She hugs me, almost too much." The bike rolls ahead, as Aston puts his feet to the pedals and cranks the gears.

"Lizzy rode this thing with you?"

Aston stands on the pedals to get better leverage, and looks at Jon hanging on tight. "I couldn't hardly get a breath. Guess she was really wantin' to sure not to fall off back dere." The bike chain clatters and the parrot squawks, as the double-mounted bike rolls on toward Stock Island.

~*~

At Key West Air Charters, the Grumman seaplane sits above the water ramp, and the smell of rich exhaust fills the air. The dual radial engines each rumble at an idle, warming up. Inside the cockpit, Rollie looks outside at Ace who stands before the left engine. The mechanic listens to the timing and then gives a thumbs up.

Coming through the front gate, the overburdened bike rattles across the empty parking lot of the fenced compound. Both Rollie and Ace watch with amusement, as the pair does a wide figure-eight then swings in toward the open hangar. Releasing his tight grip to the support bar behind the seat, Jon leaps free with his bag before Aston comes to a stop.

With a fluffy, green parrot feather stuck in his hair, Jon wobbles toward Ace at the seaplane. The mechanic takes off his baseball cap, sweeps his greying hair back to indicate that Jon should check his head, and then grunts, "Hey there, fella... I didn't think you had it in ya after the last time."

Jon grimaces and looks up to Rollie sitting in the cockpit hanging his arm out the window. The pilot grins and waves him aboard. Looking at his wristwatch, then at the mechanic, Jon asks, "Are we ready to go?"

"The client hasn't arrived yet, but the bar supplies are all loaded. Hop aboard." Ace laughs and reaches out to get the feather from Jon's hair. "No plumage required on this flight." The two walk over to the rear hatch of the seaplane, where a rolling staircase is pushed up next to the hull.

About to climb up, Jon looks back as a long, dark limousine makes the wide turn into the air charter parking lot. The vehicle swings around and parks next to Aston and the beach-trash decorated bicycle. Jon and Ace exchange a humorous look at the differing modes of transportation, and Jon comments, "I didn't pay for the ride-share upgrade."

"No, sir, you didn't." Aston waves to them, seeming to enjoy their joke as the suited client steps out of the limousine.

Jon climbs the stairway and tosses his pack inside. He looks back at Ace and salutes. "See ya in a few days."

"Take care. Oh, and don't believe a damn word of what that Julio-character tells you." The comment gives Jon pause, and he watches as Ace turns to usher the client to the plane. While Aston continues to wave farewell, Jon gets a strange feeling in his gut but shrugs it off as just being travel jitters.

VI

Moving forward toward the cockpit, Jon is greeted by Rollie. "Hey Jon, glad you could make it." He tosses the passenger a wadded-up shirt, and Jon opens the button-down garment to read the logo printed on the backside: ***Key West Air Charters – Adventure, Danger, Romance***

"What's this for?"

"Put that on, will ya."

"Why?"

"When you help out with loading the client's luggage, you will look official."

Jon bends down to look out the window and sees the gentleman in the suit walking from the limo to the airplane. Both his valet and Ace have their hands full carrying several silver travel cases. Jon leans on Rollie's armrest and questions, "What type of baggage is this?"

Eric H. Heisner

"Nothing illegal, I hope..." Rollie laughs coolly and returns to completing his preflight check. Jon slips the shirt on and makes his way to the cargo door to help with the luggage.

~*~

The rear hatch of the seaplane bangs closed, and Ace rolls the set of stairs away from the airplane. Engines revving, the seaplane rolls forward and eases down the water ramp into the gently rolling waters. A gear-churning hum echoes through the hull of the flying boat as the landing gear retracts, and the amphibious aircraft cruises out to open water.

Engines slowly throttling up, a mist of ocean spray blows back from the propellers against the V-shaped wake. Racing across the water, the seaplane gradually lifts higher, skimming the tips of the waves, and finally leaps from the water to become airborne.

At the air charter base, the limousine turns around in the parking lot and drives past the islander and his fancy bicycle. Aston gives his bird a pat, throws a leg over the bike seat and glides toward Ace at the ramp. The mechanic pushes the set of stairs aside and looks to a puddle of oil staining the pavement. He looks out to the horizon as the seaplane lifts higher in the sky and disappears amongst the clouds.

"Dey be alright-fine, mon."

Ace scuffs the toe of his boot on the oil stain. "I know. It's just that I turn into a nervous hen, when he takes my ship over international waters."

"Da seaplane fly real nice when we visit da Jamaica."

Coba Libre

The mechanic nods and smiles, wipes his hand across his mouth and starts to walk to the hangar. "You were never there, remember?"

Aston follows, walking astride his bike. "Yes, Ace-mon, sometimes it's hard to recall da places I never was."

Ace gets to the hangar door, looks to the office in back and stops. He turns to Aston, hesitates a moment, then asks, "You see Casey around lately?"

"He comes back to town with Carlos, just yesterday." Ace nods understandingly. "Rollie's been worried 'bout 'im?" The two exchange a knowing look, and Aston's bird bobs its head as the islander looks out in the direction of the marina. "He make out fine, I tink."

"Well, if he needs anything, you let me know."

"Sure ting, Ace-mon."

The mechanic waves a salute and goes into the hangar, heading for the couch next to his workbench in the back. "Aston... Now it's time for a beer and a nap..."

Watching him, Aston remains standing in the sunlit doorway, his hand stroking the parrot's head and shoulders. "See ya 'round, Mon..." Putting a foot on a pedal, he pushes off and wheels around the parking lot a few times. He circles, just for the pure fun of it, singing, "What do ya do wit a drunken sailor, what do ya do wit a drunken sailor..." With the bird on his shoulder, flapping its wings as he sings, he heads out through the front gate and pedals down the street.

~*~

The Grumman seaplane rumbles through the skies with Rollie at the controls. In the copilot chair, Jon looks out the window at puffy white clouds and the aqua-blue waters below. He adjusts the microphone on his headset and talks through the cockpit intercom, just loud enough to be heard over the steady roar of the engines. "So, who is this guy?"

Rollie turns to smile at Jon. "Just another client…"

"What's he do for work?"

"I have no idea. Didn't say, didn't ask."

Unconcerned, Rollie turns back to the controls, and Jon peeks behind at the gentleman tapping at his cell phone. Further back, the valet sits beside the stack of shiny, silver suitcases secured against the cabin wall with bungee netting. Jon faces forward again and cups his hand around the mic. "What do you think he has in all those metal cases?"

Rollie shrugs. "Who knows? Could be his toiletries, or women's undergarments for all I care."

"You're not curious?"

"Nope."

"Why not?"

Rollie casually looks over at Jon. "Everything is mostly straightforward and by the books. We fly into Cancun to clear customs and refuel. The paperwork is already filled out." Peeking past his shoulder to the cargo hold, the pilot waves when the client looks up. "I get nervous with some customers, but when they arrive with the details in order, I just figure they know what they're doing and need me to do what I know best."

"What's that?"

Coba Libre

Rollie grins. "Fly the plane and keep my mouth shut."

"Nothing shady on this deal?"

"Not really..."

Jon stares at Rollie. "What do you mean, *not really*?"

"Well, he paid in cash."

"So...?"

Rollie turns his gaze out the windscreen to the horizon. "It was a *lot* of cash."

Slumping his shoulders, Jon sinks in his seat and asks, "Is that a problem?"

"Not for me, it isn't." The pilot taps Jon on the leg. "Don't worry about it, pal." He looks at the time on his watch and hooks a thumb toward the passengers in the cargo area. "Do you mind serving the cocktails? It's about that time."

Jon looks down at the Key West Air Charters logo on his shirt pocket and frowns. "Is that the reason you wanted me to come along on this trip?"

Rollie laughs. "You're gonna have a good time, trust me. Julio is a blast..." Rollie turns his attention from the controls and gives a wink. "And there might be someone in Mexico to take your mind off that certain blonde. He has a cute cousin."

"Just one?"

Rollie smirks. "The other ones are... Let's just say, they're good cooks."

Jon laughs, as he takes off his headset, unbuckles, and eases out of the copilot seat. "Maybe a good cook is what I need. Food is the way to a man's heart."

Reaching up to adjust the dual throttles, Rollie grins, "Then some good home-cooked meals and a bit of new scenery is just what the doctor ordered."

Before exiting the cockpit to go in the back, Jon asks, "Can I get you anything?"

"I'll just have a root beer."

"How would you like that, sir?"

"On the rocks, please."

The high-winged seaplane banks southward, flying over the gulf waters toward the Yucatan Peninsula.

VII

Happy hour at the Conch Republic Tavern is a busy time. There is an even mix of tourists and local drinkers. Rays of sunlight beam inside as the front door opens and, surprisingly, a skinny kid stands silhouetted in the entryway. Casey Kettles keeps his yellow-framed sunglasses on, strutting inside as if he owns the place. He spots an unattended purse hanging from a barstool and hops on the empty seat next to it.

As he casually eyes the open bag, Angie, watching him, walks over and tosses a slice of lime, hitting him in the chest. "Don't be doing that crap in here."

Casey looks at her innocently and retorts, "Honey-pie… I'm just a dumb kid, but I know better not to shit where I eat."

Leaning on the bar, Angie talks to him above the chatter of the crowd. "Glad to see that you're back safe."

"You afraid Carlos sold me off as a slave somewhere?"

"Who'd buy you?"

"Sexual slavery perhaps?"

"Maybe after you hit puberty."

"Are you asking me on a date?"

"No, I'm hoping to sell you myself someday."

Casey smiles at Angie and lifts his sunshades, acknowledging that he has met his wit's match with her. "Carlos is okay, I guess. Just a little hung up on his Cuban thing and a certain bar-lady…"

She rolls her eyes and then scans the barroom. "Obsession is funny in that once you get what you want, you probably won't want it that much anymore."

The teenager glances toward the open purse again. "Yeah… How many wallets and gold watches can a kid have?" Next to him, the female customer notices Casey eying her handbag and lifts it from the stool defensively. He smiles at her, lets his plastic sunglasses fall back onto his nose, and smirks. "Sorry, looks like an imitation."

In a huff, she responds. "The gentleman who sold it to me said it was the real thing!"

"Of course, he did."

Offended, and not sure how to respond, the woman takes her purse and moves to the opposite side of her group. Angie stares across the bar at Casey and shakes her head. "Always the charmer…"

The kid lifts his sunglasses again and smiles gleefully. "It was real, and I bet she paid a whole shitload of money just for a stupid designer bag."

"Some folks have to buy happiness." Casey takes out a tin of tiny breath mints and offers one to Angie. She stares at him accusingly. "Did you just steal those?"

"What's the good of an expensive purse if things fall out?"

He shrugs as Angie sighs, "You want a drink?"

"Orange Fanta, please."

She grabs a glass and fills it from the soda dispenser. "Did you find anything while out there with Carlos?"

"Not really... Nothing but a whole lot of ocean water and sand to sort through... I got to do a lot of diving, though."

"You and Jorge?"

Casey snorts, "That big ape couldn't swim in a bathtub."

"No priceless treasure or pirate gold?"

"Nothing much to brag about..." He looks down the bar. "Where's that writer-guy?"

"Either he is working on his new book or took off with Rollie on a trip to Mexico."

"Are they on their honeymoon?"

She sets the soda drink down in front of him and laughs. "Very funny, smart-ass."

The boy stares at her and beams. "I'm not sure who you would be more disappointed to find out had flipped sides, Rollie or the new guy?"

"What do you mean?"

Casey rolls his eyes disgusted and takes the Jamaican treasure map out of his back pocket. "I need to return this stupid thing to Mister-wannabe-writer."

Angie unfolds the map and looks at it. "Did he lend this to you?"

"Carlos commandeered it."

"This came from Jon's lady-friend."

"Yeah, it's worthless." He looks around at the crowd. "Hey, is the writer's girlfriend around?"

"Nope... Left for the mainland..."

Casey snaps his fingers. "Dang, I thought I would show her a good time, now that I'm back."

"Sure, you would."

Flirting, the boy sips his soda straw and eyes Angie. "How about we have a good time?"

"No."

"Carlos says, *Helllooo*..." He smiles obnoxiously, and she waves him off as she goes to serve another customer.

~*~

At the Cancun International Airport, a customs agent exits the seaplane, just as a dark limousine pulls up alongside. In a moment, the client follows the valet out from the hatch and is greeted at the passenger-side door of the car by an attractive, older woman. Jon, carrying two of the polished metal suitcases, pokes his head out of the aircraft. He descends the stairway, and takes them to the limo where the driver opens the trunk. When Jon returns to the plane, Rollie hands down two more cases and follows with the rest.

As the limousine slowly pulls away, the shiny, black-tinted windows reflect Jon and Rollie standing by the seaplane. The strong smell of aircraft exhaust is thick in the air, as Jon looks around at all the private airplanes in the general aviation terminal. He comments, "That's it for the job?"

Rollie rests his elbow upon Jon's shoulder. "What were you expecting? A standoff with the Mexican Federales…?"

Relieved to not see anyone surrounding them, Jon sighs. "No… I just thought something would happen that was out of the ordinary."

Rollie turns to his airplane as the tanker truck pulls up next to the high wing. "Getting well-paid for what I do is contrary to ordinary." With a friendly nudge, Rollie gestures to the terminal building. "Let's get something to eat while they fuel us up. Tonight, we'll be in Tulum, and you'll hear all the out of the ordinary stories you can handle from my pal, Julio." As the driver of the fuel truck sets up a ladder then unwinds a length of hose, Jon and Rollie step away to get lunch.

VIII

Under blue skies, waves cascade onto a white sand beach that stretches as far as the eye can see. Where jungle meets the shore, clusters of palms overhang to shade a lineup of resort bars, filled with tables and chairs. Sitting at one of the seaside setups, a stout Mexican man sits drinking the local beer of Tulum. Nervously, he picks at the picture of the sea turtle on the label and then takes another swig from the bottle.

    A trickle of sweat streaks down his brown cheek, and he wipes it away while looking around, expecting someone. Tourists in swimsuits lay out in the sun, chat at other tables, and mill about the resort. As he finishes off his cold beverage, his stare lingers on a perky posterior belonging to an overly tan woman nearby, and he gets momentarily lost in the golden curves unfettered by skimpy beachwear.

The sudden arrival of someone to his table breaks him from his lustful trance. "Excuse me. Are you Julio Gomez?"

"Yes... Yes, I am."

Taking a stuffed envelope out of a shoulder bag, the courier drops it to the table. The two men regard each other silently, until Julio reaches over the table to open it and peek inside. Looking up, Julio speaks to the man in a hushed tone. "Terrific... You tell them just this one time, okay?"

"Is that enough payment?"

Julio takes the envelope and tucks it into his pocket. "Just this one time, understand?"

The man glances over his shoulder, and then replies, "We will be in contact soon." Without uttering another word, the courier walks back through the crowded beachfront bar, heading out toward the main street. Julio pats his pocket protectively and breathes a sigh of relief.

~*~

The Grumman seaplane's engines rumble at an idle. Slowly, they throttle up, and the plane begins to taxi forward. Through the cockpit window, Jon watches as they prepare to leave the busy Cancun airport.

Waiting for runway access, the seaplane sits behind another private charter airplane. When that aircraft takes off, the seaplane rolls ahead into position. Cleared for takeoff, Rollie reaches up to the throttles and pushes them forward. With the big radial engines roaring, the high-winged airplane races down the cleared runway and quickly lifts into the sky. Slowly, the landing gear retracts into the smooth, boat-like hull, and the plane soars into the afternoon sky.

~*~

Heading south, Rollie looks past his passenger in the copilot seat and through the window to the jungled coast of the Yucatan Peninsula. Staring, he imagines the rock cliffs and sandy beaches greeting exploring mariners of days gone by. The pilot adjusts the microphone under his chin and speaks into the intercom. "Ya know, it was over five hundred years ago that the Spanish came to conquer Mexico..." Jon gazes out the window at the coastline, as Rollie offers the history lesson. "Those guys really had some guts to cruise halfway around the world, not knowing what they were actually getting into." Enjoying the view, Jon listens. "Most folks think that Cortez conquered the Aztecs with only a few hundred soldiers."

Striking a knowing grin, Jon adds, "With the help of foreign disease spreading through the native population..."

Adjusting the fuel flow to the engines, Rollie continues, "That did a number on 'em, alright. The thing is... When you have a large reigning power, you'll always have a number of enemies who want it taken down." Reaching up, Rollie taps the overhead throttles and listens to the engines running in sync. "The Spaniards were smart in teaming up with the many local tribes that were once in alliance with the Aztecs. They had hundreds of allies and were just the small spark needed to overthrow the kingdom."

Jon ponders the concept of unrest with the local government and then comments. "I guess it was like that with the different native tribes that teamed up with England and France in their American colonies, too."

Staring ahead, Rollie nods his head and cants his jaw, lips pursed. "History goes on repeating itself again and again."

With a look of concern, Jon turns to Rollie at the controls. "What made you bring up the subject of overthrown governments and the Aztecs?"

Rollie glances at Jon and utters, "When we were at the airport, I heard news of a cartel shooting just a few days ago."

"That sort of thing happens a lot along the border."

"Yeah, well, this one was on the beaches of Cancun. They said a boat pulled up to the shore. Men with guns got out and shot down some rival gang members. Right on the beach, with the tourists around, watching…"

The color drops from Jon's features. "What…?"

Troubled, the pilot turns to him. "Nobody is happy about it. The Mexican government has called out the national guard and is trying their best to make vacationers feel safe, so you might see some Federales with machine guns around town and on the beach."

"Soldiers with guns on the beach… I don't know if that makes me feel very safe."

"When anything starts to mess with tourist dollars, they call out the big guns."

"What about the place where we're going?"

Coba Libre

"Tulum should be okay, I think. It's off the beaten path and still very rural compared to Playa del Carmen and the other coastal communities."

Jon tries to push the worrying thoughts from his mind. "I'd rather not sit on the beach with the armed forces of Mexico waiting for another cartel attack."

Rollie shrugs. "Even though you don't usually see it, that sort of business is going on all the time around here."

"I wouldn't recommend putting it on the brochure."

With a grin, the pilot announces, *"Come to the tropics! And, don't forget to bring your lawyers, guns and money…"*

Jon looks down at the Key West Air Charter logo on the shirt he's wearing. "Just like your motto promises…"

Rollie laughs and banks the seaplane toward the coast. "Wait till we hit Julio's beach… Romance is next on the list."

IX

The seaplane cruises low, just above the Caribbean waters, parallel with the white sandy beaches filled with sunbathers. Easing down into the rolling waves, out beyond the breakers, the amphibious craft makes the transition to a winged boat. Sending up sprays of water in its wake, the seaplane zips across the water's surface.

Looking out the window, Jon watches in wonder as Rollie deftly maneuvers the seaplane between the ocean swells. The pilot interrupts his focus a second to smile at Jon. "Hold on, buddy. We're going to surf it in."

Jon looks confused. "What…? Surfing?!?"

Just as an ocean swell lifts the craft, Rollie turns the tail rudder and directs the nose of the seaplane toward the beach. They dip downward as another swell raises the tail section higher and rolls past them. Rollie adjusts the engine throttles and turns the yoke. "I'll catch the next one…"

Coba Libre

This time, when the water rolls past, raising the tail, Rollie pushes both throttles forward, gunning the big engines. The plane lifts momentarily, then drops and zooms forward, carried on the crest of the ocean wave. Rollie eases back on the power, and Jon looks out the window to see a wave curling just behind the wing pontoon.

"That's where we're headed..." Rollie points to the shore where a collection of tables and chairs fill the beach in front of a palm-fringed resort. The sign on the roof reads: JULIO'S PLACE. Still riding in on the wave, Rollie eases back the throttles even more, letting the rolling waters do the work.

Jon holds tight to his seat and feels the surge of power from the ocean carrying them toward the beach. He looks over at Rollie and asks, "You do much surfing?"

"In this airplane, I do. It's best to ride a good wave in, or it can get rough trying to time a landing between breakers on the beach." As the hull scrapes into the sandy bottom, Rollie turns to Jon with a smirk. "When the tail goes up, the nose goes down. If you get hit with the next wave wrong. Over you go..." Rollie activates the landing gear, and the seaplane slowly rolls up out of the water, onto the shore.

"Nice landing... Both times."

The seaplane rolls up on the wet sand, and one engine cuts back as the other revs up, pivoting the water bird around to face out to open water again. A stout man runs from the beach bar, waving his hand in greeting and displaying a welcoming grin. Leaning over, Rollie returns the wave through Jon's window. "And there is Julio…"

~*~

Sand ceases blowing across the beach, as the seaplane's engines choke to a halt. Julio stands outside the plane's rear hatch and waits until the door opens. Popping his head out, Rollie greets his old friend with a smile. The pilot looks down at the vacant patch of beach and asks, "Is it okay to park here?"

Waving to a yard boy standing by with a coil of rope, Julio exclaims, "Yes, Rollie! We will tie-off your plane to a tree, my good friend, so it is still here when high tide comes in."

Lashing an end of the rope to a palm tree, the boy trots over with the loose coil to tie-off the seaplane. Rollie hops down from the hatch and receives a fond embrace from Julio. Catching his breath after the spine-popping hug, Rollie puts his hands on Julio's shoulders to regard his friend. "Been a while. Good to see you too, old pal!"

When Jon peeks his head out from the hatch, Julio looks up at him. "Who is your copilot?"

The pilot turns to his plane and offers an introductory gesture, "This here is Jon Springer. He's an aspiring writer who recently moved to Key West, looking for some inspiration."

Julio waves him down. "Greetings from the Yucatan… We have much inspiration here, for miles! Mayan ruins, beaches, bikinis, and cenotes…"

Jumping to the sand from the seaplane hatch, Jon replies, "I'm familiar with all of those except cenotes."

Rollie pipes in. "Underground rivers…"

"Yes, a whole system of underground water flows beneath our land here in Quintana Roo." Julio stomps the sand under his feet. "Well, not on the beach, exactly… But inland, through the jungle, there are ponds and rivers that disappear deep underground, forming caves that connect to each other, miles apart."

"I've never heard of a cenote."

"There are thousands, all around Mexico, with many of the most beautiful ones located right here on the peninsula." Julio waves his hand for them to follow. "I forget my manners. First, let's get you both something to drink. I will show you my photo album of underground rivers, and you will tell me what you would like to do on your visit."

Standing beside his airplane, Rollie gestures for Jon to go along with their host. "Go ahead. I'll see that my bird here is nested proper and meet up with you guys in a bit." Rollie mutters a few words of Spanish to the boy with the tether line, and Jon, following after Julio, makes his way through the sand toward the beach bar.

X

The expansive row of windows in Julio's office frames the beach and the evening skyline. The decor of the room is assembled like a museum of Mayan culture, containing shelves and tables overflowing with a mix of tourist trinkets and historical artifacts. A distinct smell of incense attempts to cover the odor of objects that could be hundreds of years old.

Sitting in a chair fashioned out of driftwood and leather, Jon sips from a cocktail. He watches Julio thumb through the pages of a big, palm-covered photo album, smiling as he goes. The host turns the book and displays a photo of a watery cave that opens out to the jungle. Rays of sunlight filter artfully across the picture of a bikini-clad woman perched on a ledge and ready to dive into the pool. Julio points to the photograph. "This is one of the many cenotes you will find around Tulum."

Jon takes a drink and comments, "Nice scenery."

Quick on the uptake, Julio grins proudly. "Yes, yes… She is one of my girlfriends."

Glancing around at the clutter of the private collection, Jon jokes, "Not married, I assume?"

The gregarious host turns the book back to himself and flips some pages. "I was married once, when I was young. Nobody told me the truth about women, and I had to find everything out the hard way."

"Most of us do."

Reminiscing, Julio sighs. "She was the most beautiful girl a boy of seventeen had ever laid eyes upon, and in only a few short years, turned into a very nasty, ugly woman that disliked me very much."

Jon, continuing to take in the room of primitive relics and artwork, distractedly remarks, "Some say marriage is an expensive way to watch someone slowly grow to dislike you…"

Flipping pages, Julio's eyes light up with excitement, and he turns the book around to Jon again. "Ahh, this is a wonderful one nearby that maybe I can take you to while you are here." The photo shows another jungle-framed cenote, amazingly more beautiful than the first. There is a bikini-clad woman in this one, as well, more gorgeous than the last.

Jon's head bobs, as he stares at the exotic photograph. "Very beautiful…"

Julio laughs and peeks over the top of the album to get a better look at the photograph. "Yes, she is."

"Another girlfriend?"

"I take great pleasure to share each place of beauty in nature with a different female companion. The only trick of it is to keep straight which special place belongs to whom?" Grinning, Julio turns the page. "Yes, this photograph book has kept me out of trouble many times." He turns the page toward Jon and shows an interesting cenote with a woman who is more average-looking. "This is one of my favorites."

Jon tilts his head to better appreciate the unique locale. "I would really enjoy checking out one of these cenotes."

Turning the book back to himself, Julio smiles warmly. "This was my most favorite and easily the loveliest woman." He looks up at Jon and asks, "Don't you think?"

Jon takes another look and shrugs. "Is she your sister? The other ones were a bit more eye-catching."

"No, she is of no relation." The gaiety drops from Julio's face, and he openly asks, "Have you been married?"

About to take another sip from his drink, Jon hesitates, sensing the changed mood by the serious tone of the question. "Uh, no… The right woman hasn't found me yet."

"This one has not the outward beauty of the others, but she had a sparkle in her eyes that mere beauty cannot surpass." Jon gazes down at the photo again as Julio continues. "Kindness is a beauty that feeds a man's soul. Believe you me, I meet many an attractive woman who only cares for herself, and the outer shell quickly fades. When she looks at you with sparkling eyes that speak of kindness and understanding… That is the most beautiful woman in the world."

"Looks only go so far."

Julio flips more pages. "Yes, they are a nice distraction, but they eventually age." Laughing, the small-statured man stands to his full five feet. "Fortunately for the male species, women often look for qualities in men other than his looks." Julio pats his bulky torso and puts on his distinctive look of quirky charm. "Women age and grow older, while men who never grow up only become more distinguished."

Thinking of his time with Lizzy, Jon feels a surge of emotions and a sense of loss. He sweeps his hand through his hair and thinks on the first sightings of grey that he's seen recently. The album is turned to Jon again, and Julio shows off another cenote with a woman wearing only the bikini bottom. "This one was very, very beautiful, but had no depth."

Admiring the rich scenery in the tasteful photograph, Jon finishes off his drink just as there is a knock at the door. Julio places the book in Jon's lap and hustles over to answer it. He peeks out and then opens the door wide to reveal Rollie, who spots the familiar photo album in Jon's lap and grins. "Showing off one of your famous picture books?"

Jon looks surprised. "There's more than one?"

"Oh, yeah... Julio has more of those photo albums than girlfriends. He spout off any outrageous lies about me yet?"

Ushering the pilot inside, Julio closes the door behind. "We only talk about women. You don't know women much, so we can talk about you, now that you are here."

Rollie looks around the office at the enormous collection of local art. "Wow, your collection has really grown."

"It is like a magnet of nature. These things come to me to be their caretaker."

"And dealer…"

Julio smiles. "Yes, some of these items want me to increase my wealth by finding them the right home."

After examining a painting leaned against the wall, Rollie looks over to see Jon thumbing through the photo album. He looks to Julio and grins knowingly. "The cenote book…?"

Their host goes to the bar and speaks over his shoulder. "Purely for educational purposes…" He starts to mix another round of drinks and asks, "Rollie, my friend… What sort of beverage would you like?"

"What about some food?"

Julio clinks ice cubes into three glasses and begins to pour a mixed concoction over each. "We will be dining tonight with one of my cousin's family." Rollie grins and exchanges a comical look with Jon. Handing one of the cocktails to Rollie, Julio catches the obvious expression and remarks to them both, "Yes, I see you have mentioned something about my cousins. This one has a lot of extra beauty… Mostly all on the inside." He winks at Jon. "You could say, she is overstuffed with it."

The three have a laugh. Jon raises his glass and toasts, "Cheers to the many types of women in many forms of beauty."

Rollie quickly catches on to the prior conversation and lifts his drink. "Cheers to that."

Coba Libre

Taking a long swallow, Julio nearly finishes his drink. He sets the glass aside and goes to his desk. "It is not too far. How would we like to go?"

Jon looks puzzled and Rollie asks, "Do you mean, walk or drive?"

"Too far to walk. Pedal bikes or bar shuttle?"

Jon sits with his drink in hand. "I already had a wild ride on a bicycle this morning. My vote is for the bar shuttle."

Julio grins, as he pulls out a single key from the desk drawer. "I like your sense of adventure!" Their host goes back to grab his drink, finishes it and then trots to the doorway. "Come along now... Our journey awaits!"

Jon and Rollie exchange a mutual look of concern. Getting up, Jon whispers to him. "What *is* the bar shuttle?"

"I'm not really too sure... He is a wheeler-dealer of sorts, so it could be anything." Carrying their drinks, the two follow Julio outside, and the door is pulled shut behind.

XI

Julio unlocks a padlock on an old, metal-covered outbuilding and unfastens the rusty chain that secures the two barn doors. He swings the sagging doors open and steps into the dark shed. Moving forward to peek inside, Jon and Rollie are momentarily blinded as a set of bright headlights blink on. A cloud of exhaust billows from the shed, as a diesel engine cranks, sputters, then rumbles to life. Jon and Rollie both step back to catch a breath of fresh air. Blinking and coughing, Jon waves his hand past his face. "What the heck is that?"

Rollie pronounces, *"It's aliiiive!!!"* They move to the side, as the 1950's, military-model Dodge Power-wagon pulls out from the shed. The rust-patina gives the boxy truck a vintage character that shows its many years of service. Rollie laughs, as Julio drives out next to them. "Only you would drive around town in this thing."

Eric H. Heisner

Inside, Julio pats the metal dashboard affectionately. "Rollie, my friend... I got a deal on it, and it goes anywhere."

The exhaust fumes lessen considerably as the engine warms up, and Jon has a realization. "This is the bar shuttle? Julio, it looks more like a transport truck from *Indiana Jones*."

Their host grins broadly. "Every ride is an adventure!" Rollie and Jon walk around to the door on the passenger side. With a loud creak, Julio wrenches the warped metal door open and waves them aboard. "Boss-man sits in the middle."

Jon looks at Rollie confused, and the pilot waves him in. "That's you... Hop in." As Jon climbs into the vintage truck, he looks at Rollie. "Why am *I* the boss?"

Rollie climbs in and pulls the door shut with a creaking-bang. "*You* don't have to drive or get out to open the gate."

In the middle, scrunched on the bench seat, Jon sits looking out through the cracked, flat, split-panel windshield. He looks at Julio, who feathers the gas pedal to keep the engine running. "Is this thing safe to ride in?"

The driver laughs and jams the shifter in gear. "I toss drunken tourists in the back to take to other hotels all the time."

Jon peers over his shoulder and through the window at the rusty truck bed behind them. "I'll stay up front with you." Julio jams his sandaled foot on the gas pedal. The engine roars as he releases the clutch, and the truck lunges forward.

Coba Libre

Partly paved and mostly dirt, the truck bounces through enormous potholes that would swallow up most other vehicles. The powerful headlights shine a bright clear path through the swarms of tourists crowding the road. Gripping the skinny, oversized steering wheel, Julio smiles at his passengers and laughs. "We like to keep tourists off our roads. If an unfamiliar driver hits one of these bottomless pits wrong, they turn in the keys to their rental car, and never want to drive here again."

Jon bounces back and forth, as Julio maneuvers the truck along the uneven roadway. Holding onto the dashboard with both hands to steady himself, Jon queries, "Why don't they fill in the holes?"

Julio cranks the wheel and veers around another water-filled crater. "They do, but then they are back a few days later. It is a part of life and adds a bit of charm, don't you think?"

Jon's head is snapped to the side, as they dip into another one. He pushes back against the seat and mutters, "Yeah, charming..."

In good humor, Julio turns to his two passengers and chides them. "Relax... You must loosen up. When you are stiff, it makes the ride much worse."

Rollie holds tight to the door handle, and Jon looks over his shoulder to the truck bed. "When drunk tourists are hauled around in the back of this, are *they* relaxed enough?"

The Mexican driver jokes. "Some get so comfortable that they will sometimes pass out. The ones that don't are usually puking over the side."

61

Eric H. Heisner

Jon braces himself and nods. "I can relate…"

Rollie raps his knuckles on the rusty metal door panel. "Julio, this is just the kind of vehicle you should be driving."

The driver suddenly slams on the brakes. Standing on the pedal, he lifts in the seat to peer over the hood of the truck. He waves his hand and hollers, "Out of the way, you chicken!!! You nearly became our dinner!" He pushes on the emblem at the center of the steering wheel, and a blast from a trucker's air-horn scatters the clucking poultry to the side the road. Julio turns to see his passengers' surprised reaction and grins. "Ordered the horn special from Buc-ee's truck stop in Tejas, and I installed it myself." Julio points to a house, glowing with colored lights, on the coastal side of the road, and exclaims, "That's my cousin's place!" Shifting the truck into a lower gear, they turn down a dirt path, just off the main road.

In front of the modest, shanty-style beach house, the old truck sputters to a halt and shuts off. Outdoor lights glow in the darkness, as Latin music cascades through the open windows. The three climb out of the truck, and Rollie pats his stomach. "You're gonna really love his cousin's home-cooked meal, Jon. Best Mexican food you'll ever have…"

As his own stomach growls, Jon follows them to the front door. "I haven't had good Mexican food since leaving California for the Keys."

Julio turns to Jon. "You call that pig slop Mexican food?" He stops to give Jon a scolding look. "You have *not* had authentic Mexican food if you've only had it in California."

Jon smiles apologetically. "I've been to Cabo.... *Twice.*"

Their host waves a dismissive hand and ushers them along. Pushing the front door open, he hollers, "Hola, Marta! Rollie and a friend are here. They are hungry, and the friend has *never* had Mexican food!!!" They enter the home, and the door swings closed to the beat of local music.

XII

On the back veranda of the house, the meal has been cleared. The two guests sit contented, each holding a cold beverage, relaxing while admiring the ocean view and the starry skies. Julio arrives with three long cigars. He hands one to Rollie, sticks one in his mouth, and offers the remaining one to Jon. "This is how to enjoy your first night in Mexico."

Rollie takes a wooden match from a tray on the table, strikes it on the underside of his chair and watches it flare up. He rolls the end of the cigar on the flame and takes a puff. "Livin' the good life, I see."

Julio lights a match and scoots the tray over toward Jon. "My financial situation has improved very much since our puddle-jumping days down in Panama."

Rollie holds the lit cigar and blows a cloud of smoke. "When you're on the bottom, there is no place to go but up."

The Mexican lights his own cigar, pinches it between his thumb and fingers, and points it at Rollie. "We could've been set up a lot sooner, if you had wanted to take more risks."

Rollie takes a few puffs, while Jon lights a match and listens to their conversation. The seaplane pilot gazes out at the dark ocean waves and contemplates, "Life is all about choices, and I chose not to live mine in jail."

"They didn't *all* go to jail."

"Yeah… *Some* of them are *dead*."

Smoke wisps out from Julio's nostrils, and he coughs. "You still have that crusty ol' Jiminy Cricket sitting on your shoulder to keep you from getting in trouble?"

Holding the cigar between his thumb and forefinger, Rollie looks to the orange, glowing end and nods. "Who, Ace? I stay out of a fair share of trouble and still keep him busy."

Julio puffs a few times and blows out a cloud of smoke. "He's a damn good mechanic."

"Yes, he is."

As Jon sits back to enjoy his own cigar, quietly observing the friendly reunion, Julio looks to Jon and then at Rollie. "Business is good in Key West, no?"

"I mostly get by… This trip will pay a few bills."

Julio laughs. "Sí, the stars must be aligning for us both, as I have made a profitable deal in the last few days as well."

Rollie looks at Julio suspiciously. "Should I be worried?"

"No… It is only a local thing. No harm to anyone."

"I heard what happened in Cancun the other day."

"Yes, the big cartels have been challenged by small-time dealers, and they are trying to enforce their dominance."

"Doesn't look good…"

"It happens often, but it was in poor taste to execute their plans in front of the tourists. There will be soldiers everywhere for a good while, until the news is forgotten."

Rollie knocks the ash off his cigar and examines the end. "How are things down here?"

"We are merely a simple Mayan beach community, away from the many problems of the big cities. We are cautious, but so far have been untouched by such issues."

They puff away, enjoying fine cigars while gazing up at the starry night sky. Jon waves a cloud of smoke from his face and comments, "Why would the cartel make such a violent display on a crowded beach, when most of their drug war battlegrounds are on the U.S. border and in Mexico City?"

Julio continues to stare skyward and casually replies, "The same reason they do anything."

Coba Libre

"Money?"

The Mexican's gaze darts to Jon. "Yes, and power..."

"Who was challenging the cartels in the Yucatan?"

Julio glances at Rollie and then turns to address Jon. "There are always other tiny fish lurking, waiting to move up. Offshore, millions of dollars of merchandise move every night. Like the police, even the cartels cannot monitor the vast waters of the Gulf effectively. When too much gets through, and it becomes noticeable, they send their enforcers around to remind the small fish who they are dealing with."

"Sounds like it can get pretty violent."

"That is the way of business dealings in the whole world. As it has been for thousands of years... The characters change, but the story remains the same."

Jon holds his cigar, licks his teeth and takes a breath. "Throughout time, there have only been a few original stories, and we just replay them, repeating history."

Julio puffs on his cigar, ashes it and nods his head. "Rollie tells me you are a writer."

"I work at it."

"Ahh... Yes, the creative artist must labor at his craft, and if he works long and hard enough, he will fool everyone into thinking that it takes no effort at all."

Jon responds, "The blessing and curse of creativity."

Their leisurely smoking and drinking continues, while staring at the bright star-lit skies over the dark ocean waters. Just below the horizon, there is a sudden flash of light followed by the thundering bang of an explosion. As Jon stares at the glowing spot on the water, Rollie turns to Julio accusingly, uttering, "Damn..."

Jon blinks his eyes and turns to them. "What was *that*?" Pointing at the horizon, he asks, "Did you *see* that?"

Julio fidgets with his cigar and bites his lip nervously. "Was only lightning, possibly..."

Snuffing his cigar in the tray, Rollie shakes his head and murmurs under his breath. "Lightning, my ass..."

Jon's gaze returns to the faraway spot where a faint glow remains. "It looked like an explosion."

Julio taps the ash from his cigar and shakes his head. "Just an optical illusion..."

Surprised, Jon turns to Julio, wondering if he's joking. "It sure sounded like an explosion to me." A cell phone rings, and Julio nearly jumps out of his skin. Jon watches as Julio takes the mobile device from his pocket, looks at the caller's number, gets up and moves away to answer it.

Rollie watches him leave the patio, finishes his drink and then looks to Jon. "Let's wrap it up. We'll get a night's sleep and then head out early tomorrow morning."

Peering out into the darkness, Jon tries to identify whatever it was that made the flash of light. "What *was* that?" When Rollie scoots back his chair, Jon turns to him as if he just heard his previous remark. He asks, "I thought we were going to stay a few days?"

"Something just came up, and we should be getting back."

Jon looks confused. "Really?"

"I don't want to keep you from finishing the work on your book."

Jon takes another drag on his cigar, exhales, and continues to stare intently into the distance at the dark ocean. "That's okay... I sent what I had to my agent before we left. He'd be pestering me every single day I was here, if I left town without sending him something."

"How would he know where you were?"

Jon sits back in his chair, thinks and shakes his head. "Heck, I have no idea, but he *always* finds me."

"I really appreciate you tagging along on this trip. Maybe we could camp along the Dry Tortugas on the way back home to Key West and do some fishing."

Puffing on his cigar, Jon nods. "Fine by me." He glances to the spot on the ocean again and then looks around for Julio. "What about our host?"

"I'm not sure where he went, but he could be a while. Let's head back without him."

"How?"

Rollie gets up from his seat and offers a roguish grin. "He left the key in the truck."

"How will Julio get back?"

Rollie shrugs, heads to the house and calls back to Jon. "He always figures something out..."

XIII

Through the night, Julio's truck rumbles down the bumpy main road back toward the beach resort. The dimly lit streets are mostly empty after the bars and restaurants have closed. Holding tight onto the door handle as they bounce along, Jon notices that there is a much wealthier class of business in Tulum than the surrounding areas.

"I guess the locals don't eat at most of these places?"

Rollie swerves the truck around a water-filled crater in the middle of the roadway. "No, it's mostly wealthy tourists, and the locals only work there."

"I thought Tulum was getting known as a remote location for eco-tourism."

"Yep, when you slap the label *eco-tourism* on the sign, you just raised the price so the locals can't afford it anymore."

They arrive at Julio's place, and Rollie pulls the truck up to park in front of the doors of the metal garage. Jon looks around at the modest resort. "Julio seems to be doing okay."

"Yeah, *seems* to be..." Rollie steps from the truck and speaks across the cab to Jon. "I'm going to check on the plane. Get some sleep, and we'll head out at first light."

Jon gets out and walks to the back of the truck bed, calling after Rollie, "Where do I sleep?"

Already halfway to the beach, Rollie hollers back, "We're in suite number two. Second door down the hallway, to the left of his office. They already put your bag in there."

Jon sees that the resort has its accent lights turned on. Just enough to find your way, but not enough to contribute to light pollution... He waves at a security guard sitting in the shadows and enters the main lobby.

Walking past Julio's office, Jon notices there is a light coming from under the door. He stops, looks at the late hour on his wristwatch and then decides to knock. There is no answer, and he turns the doorknob to find it locked. Leaning in closer, he listens and gives another tap on the door.

When there is no response, Jon continues down the hallway to find his room. Not having a key, he knocks on the door to the suite, gives the knob a turn and finds it unlocked. He gently pushes the door open, peeks inside and whispers, "Hello, anyone...?" The door swings inward and Jon enters.

~*~

Coba Libre

A few hours later, Jon lays sprawled out on one of the two beds in the beach resort suite, with most of his clothes on. His open bag sits on the bedside dresser with only a few items unpacked. With a grunting snore, he rolls over, scrunches the pillow and wipes a bit of drool from his cheek.

Through an opening in the partially closed curtains, the sky is dark, and a garden spotlight directed over at the palm trees illuminates a portion of the beach near Rollie's seaplane. With the rising tide, gentle waves reach further up the beach and wash away sandy footprints near the curved hull.

Aside from the soft snore of slumber, the room is quiet. The click of the door latch and the slow creak of hinges breaks the stillness, announcing someone's arrival. Still half-asleep, Jon lifts his head and looks toward the dark lingering figure in the doorway. "Rollie…?"

The door clicks closed, and the shadowy form moves swiftly toward Jon's bedside. Before Jon can make out who it is, the person whispers, "You must pack up and be on your way, my friend. It is not safe for you here."

Roused from his sleep, Jon sits up and looks around. "What…?" Dazed, he asks, "Is that you, Julio?"

"Yes, but where is Rollie?"

"He was checking on the airplane."

"Good, then you will be ready to depart shortly."

Jon looks at the window and the dark sky outside. "What time is it?"

"Time to go."

Clicking on the lamp, Jon blinks to let his eyes adjust as he slowly wakes. He picks up his wristwatch from the dresser, puts it on and squints at the time. "Where's Rollie?"

Gathering Jon's items, Julio packs them into the bag. "You said he was at the airplane."

"Yeah, but that was hours ago."

Julio stops stuffing items in the bag, and looks at Jon. "When did you see him last?"

"We got back here sometime after two or so."

Julio rushes to the window and looks out at the beached seaplane, as the predawn sky starts to lighten. "You have not seen him since?" They both look to the other bed in the room, untouched with Rollie's bag sitting on top.

Jon shakes his head, suddenly awake. "No…"

"Grab your stuff and come with me." On the way out, Julio grabs Rollie's bag, and Jon follows him out the door.

XIV

Jon follows Julio, out through the empty beach bar and onto the shore where the seaplane is tethered. He watches Julio toss Rollie's bag inside the rear cargo door before taking a look inside and then scanning the length of the dark beach. Perplexed, Jon stands behind the airplane, as Julio remarks, "He's not here."

"I see that."

"That's not good…"

"What do you mean? Where could he be?"

Julio searches the sand around the seaplane for clues. "You must be going now."

"Why?"

"Certain business situations have gone awry, and it is not safe to have you or the seaplane here any longer."

"What about Rollie?"

Coba Libre

As the morning sky brightens, Julio examines several sets of different footprints in the sand. Head down, he follows them around the plane until they meet and get mixed together. Jon follows, and pauses when he sees a set of heel-drag marks leading up the beach. The two stop and exchange a look of concern. Jon tries to rub the sleep from his eyes, as if trying to wake from a nightmare. "I see it, but I don't believe it."

"This is no bueno."

"They took Rollie?"

Julio toes the footprints in the sand and then turns to Jon. "Do you know how to fly this plane out of here?"

"No."

Julio stares seriously at Jon for a moment before turning his gaze to the airplane. "If they take the seaplane, it is as good as gone forever."

"Who would take it?"

"The people who just were here and took our friend Rollie."

"Why would they take him?"

Wringing his hands, Julio walks to the airplane hatch. He stops and looks back to Jon. "They will keep him alive, until they persuade him to fly or find someone else who will do it."

"Who are these people?"

"Bad people... Very bad people."

The morning sun starts to crest over the horizon, brightening the sky. Jon kicks into the sand, shakes his head, and grumbles, "I can't believe this…"

At the rear hatch of the seaplane, Julio searches inside a side pocket of Rollie's duffle bag and pulls out a pen and paper. He scribbles something down, along with a set of numbers, and tears off the note. "Go to this address. Don't talk to anyone else, and I will meet you there in a day or so."

Jon takes the scrap of paper and looks at it. "Really...? Are you kidding?" He watches, as Julio unfastens the tether line from the tail section, tosses the loose end of the rope up the beach and circles the airplane. "Where are *you* going?"

"I will see you soon."

"Shouldn't I stay with the plane and go with you?"

Julio shakes his head and climbs inside the cargo hold. "No, it will be safer for you there." He swings the hatch door shut with a soft clank, fastens the latch and makes his way up through the cargo area toward the cockpit.

Jon watches Julio sit behind the controls, pull on a headset and begin the preflight checklist. Uncertain of his safety on the beach, he looks at the note in hand and mutters, "Where...? I hardly know where *here* is."

As the radial engines engage, Jon is blinded by the sunlight cresting the horizon. Shielding his eyes from the glare, Jon feels a grit of sand blow back from the spinning propellers. Drowned out by the roar of engines, Jon yells at the airplane, "But, I don't want to stay!"

The seaplane slides off the beach and chugs through the crashing waves. Out past the breakers, the engines throttle up. The flying boat skims along the surface, until it leaps into the sky, banks to the east, and flies away from the coastline. Bewildered, Jon stares at the seaplane until it is out of sight.

He looks at the scrap of paper in his hand again, and reads the address and phone number that Julio jotted down. Turning the message over, he stares at the blank backside. "Where the heck is Akumal?" From behind, someone startles him, and Jon turns to see a young boy laden with dozens of woven trinkets and tourist items.

"That is where the turtles come in."

"Turtles…?"

"Sí, Señor…" The boy makes the motion of swimming. "Many turtles to see in Akumal."

Jon nods and scans the lengthy beach in both directions. "Which way?"

When the boy points north, Jon considers it a moment and starts walking. Hearing the boy giggle behind him, he turns around. "You said this way?"

"*Señor Borrachón…* No walk. Too far. Take autobus."

"How far?"

"Mucho kilometers."

"Okay, thanks." He adjusts the pack on his shoulder. "I'll figure something out." Jon clutches the note and walks up the beach to Julio's place. Behind him, the young boy calls out. "Would you like to buy a souvenir?"

"Not today, gracias…" Jon looks at the note again and considers the phone number written under the address. Proceeding across the beach, through the closed patio bar area, he heads toward Julio's private office.

XV

The door is unlocked. Warily, Jon enters and looks around the vacant office. Making his way to the desk, he reaches over the clutter of Mayan artifacts, lifts the phone from its cradle and taps in a number.

The phone rings twice and there is an answer on the other end of the line. *"Conch Republic Tavern, Key West…"*

"Hello, Angie…? It's Jon Springer."

The poor connection makes her voice seem faraway. "Hey there, Jon! How's the vacation going?"

"Uh, it was okay at first…"

"I can barely hear you."

"Yeah, uh, Rollie was kidnapped."

The line crackles, and Angie's voice comes in faintly. "What was that Jon? We have a bad connection!"

"Rollie was kidnapped."

"What?"

"They took Rollie."

"Where is he…?"

"I don't know."

"What about his pal, Julio?"

Jon looks around the office and then down at the note. "He left and only gave me a local number with an address." There is a brief silence on the other end of the phone call. Finally, Angie shushes someone nearby and adds, "Sorry Jon… It's loud in here, and I can't hear you very well."

"Have you heard from him by any chance?"

The call fades then returns with Angie's voice staticky. "I haven't heard anything, but I can check with Ace."

"Okay, thanks… What should I do?"

"I'd give the number a try, and maybe you…" The call disconnects, and Jon hears static, followed by a dial tone. Clicking the phone off, Jon sits and looks around Julio's office. He takes a breath and then, reading the number on the paper, dials it on the keypad. The telephone line is quiet for a moment, then rings. A woman answers, and Jon is surprised to hear a female voice again on the other end of the line. "Angie…?"

"No, this is Rebecca Vargas."

"Uh, hello."

"Hello."

"Sorry to bother you… I was given this number."

"By whom?"

"Julio."

"And who is this?"

Coba Libre

"My name is Jon Springer."

There is a long pause and then, "Okay…?"

Wiping beads of sweat from his forehead, Jon states, "I'm on a trip here in Mexico with a friend, Rollie McKinny." At the mention of the aviator, the woman's voice perks up. "Rollie is in town?"

"He was, but we can't find him now."

"Try looking for him at the seaplane."

"We already did that, and he's gone."

She laughs good-humoredly and replies, "Hang around that plane of his long enough, and he'll show up."

Unsure of how much actually to tell her, Jon stutters, "Julio just left in Rollie's seaplane."

"Where did he go?"

"I don't know."

"Why are you calling me?"

"He gave this number and an address."

"Is the address in Akumal?"

"Yes."

"Well, don't come here."

Jon gulps and turns to look out the picture window. "Where should I go?"

"Where are you now?"

"In Julio's office…"

"When did he give you the note?"

"Just before he left."

There is a sigh and a short pause on the telephone line. "How long ago did he leave?"

"About fifteen, maybe twenty minutes ago…"

"You better get away from there if he said you should. Go to the ruins of Tulum, and I will meet you there shortly."

The phone line suddenly disconnects, and the dial tone pulses in Jon's ear. He looks at the receiver, hangs it up and stares at the artifacts on the desk. After taking a calming breath, he pushes back Julio's chair and grabs his bag. Eyeing the room for some sort of weapon to defend himself with, he spots a Mayan ceremonial knife with an obsidian blade and carved figure on the handle. He picks it up, weighs it in his hand, holds it out in front and stabs the air, performing a comical exercise of self-defense. With a shrug, he tucks the dagger in his bag and mutters, "I prefer when they give me the old-fashioned pistol."

~*~

The beach resort is just starting to wake for the day, as ground crews clean up fallen sticks and leaves. Jon walks to Julio's parked truck, peers through the driver's window and sees the key in the ignition. He pulls open the door and climbs inside the old truck.

Looking behind over the rusty truck bed to the roadway, he notices a pair of black SUVs, with dark-tinted windows, pull up in front of Julio's place. Several men in sport-leisure attire step out with wrapped bundles tucked under their arms. Watching them closely, Jon sees that at least one of the men is concealing a snub-nosed machine gun.

"Oh, crap...!" Jon immediately ducks down behind the steering wheel and waits until they have passed from sight. Pressing his foot on the clutch pedal, he turns the ignition key. The engine cranks loudly, over and over, trying to start. Peeking over the dashboard, Jon taps the gas pedal until, finally, the motor roars to life.

Shifting the truck into reverse, Jon turns to look out the rear window toward the street. As the truck rolls backward, one of the sport-suited men suddenly appears behind it. Raising an automatic machine gun to chest level, he calls out, "Alto, muchacho!" Jon sees the weapon, panics, and punches his foot on the gas pedal.

The high bumper at the rear of the truck hits the man mid-thigh and plows over him. Jon curses under his breath and keeps his foot on the gas. The truck races backward into the street and smacks broadside into one of the black SUVs. Both vehicles skid across the dirt roadway, until they smash into the other SUV, pinning it against a shaggy palm.

Shifting gears, Jon pulls forward and looks to see the man he just ran over sitting up between a pair of tire tracks. Seemingly uninjured, the man looks at his fallen weapon, broken in half and crushed into the ground. He picks up the busted pieces and yells an alert to the others. "Aquí!!! Aquí!!!

"Holy shit...!" Jon hammers his foot on the gas pedal, cranks the steering wheel and drives ahead. In his side mirror, he sees the group of men crowd around the smashed vehicles and then point up the road in his direction. The truck jolts hard, as it splashes through a watery crater in the road. Jon turns his attention forward and tries to avoid more potholes, as he drives down the crowded street. He swerves around a group of tourists on bicycles and then comes to a stop behind a long line of mud-spattered cars and delivery trucks.

Jon glances to his mirrors again. "Crap, crap, crap...!" He sees the group of men, a short distance away, stop pointing and start walking toward him. They break into a jog, keeping their guns tucked out of view. Jon sits waiting, stuck in traffic, his eyes darting to the stalled vehicles ahead and then to the men advancing from behind.

Sweat streams down Jon's temples, as he debates abandoning Julio's vehicle or waiting for the traffic to move. Now, with the approaching men only a few cars back, he looks to the vehicles ahead and gingerly taps on the air horn. Everyone on the street stops in their tracks. When Jon looks back to the advancing men, he notices one of them flash a wicked grin.

Getting a lot of attention now, Jon decides to stick it out and begins to press the air horn repeatedly. He reaches across the truck cab to lock the passenger door and, when he sits upright again, he is greeted by a man, with a military rifle and outfitted in urban-camo, standing at his driver-side window.

"Pardon, Señor?"

After the initial startle, Jon cranks down the window and greets the Mexican soldier with his very limited Spanish. "Que?"

"Disculpe la demora, pero el tráfico se moverá pronto."

Jon nods, not understanding, and replies, "Gracias."

Coba Libre

The soldier looks inside the truck to Jon's backpack on the seat and then studies the outside of the old military vehicle. "Este es un gran camión viejo, pero tocar esa bocina no ayuda realmente a la situación."

Jon looks outside to see that, because of the military presence, the men following have moved off to blend in with the sidewalk crowd. He smiles at the soldier at his window. "Sí… Gracias. Gracias."

"No entiendes español?"

Jon bobs his head as if he understands, and then speaks slowly to the soldier in English. "I - am - trying - to - get - to - the - ruins - of -Tulum… Mayan ruins…." Jon makes gestures, trying to convey the impression of several pyramids, which looks more like he is outlining the curves of the female figure.

The soldier looks at him strangely and then replies in perfect American English. "If you're looking to find the ruins, keep straight on this road and take a right at the highway. Follow the signs."

"Gracias. Gracias Señor."

The soldier shakes his head, notices that traffic is now moving and waves him along. As the Mexican sergeant steps back from the truck, Jon shifts into gear, gives a feeble salute and drives off. He looks to his rearview mirror and sees one of the sport-suited thugs at the edge of the sidewalk crowd, avoiding attention from the nearby soldiers.

XVI

Arriving at the ruins before the park gates open, Jon pulls up to the entrance. Along the road leading to the front entrance, vendors are just starting to set up their booths to sell food and souvenirs to the tourists. He stops, letting the old truck idle, while he looks around for anyone who is expecting to meet him.

Shifting into gear, Jon drives forward and cruises through the empty parking lot. He turns into a spot at the edge of the lot, facing out to the street for a quick and easy getaway. With the noise of the engine still drumming in his ears, he sits in silence after pulling the key from the ignition. "Nobody here. I guess I'll just wait…"

~*~

Near the entrance gate, while keeping an eye out for the woman he is supposed to meet, Jon pretends to read at an information kiosk. As he scans the captions, a large group of Chinese tourists swarm around the exhibit, crowding him out. At a loss for what to do next, he walks toward the entrance gate and suddenly hears his name.

"Señor Springer..."

Jon turns around to see a short Mexican man with only a few stubby teeth. The old man's dark eyes squint as he grins, holding up a display board of jewelry for sale.

"Hello. Rebecca...?"

The little man laughs with a high-pitched chortle and steps aside to reveal an attractive Mexican woman with long, dark hair pulled back in a ponytail. In shock, she looks at the old man and back to Jon. "Did you think that was *me*?"

Embarrassed, Jon offers a feeble shrug. "I don't know... I just heard someone say my name."

Offended, her jaw drops. "Is *that* what you pictured when we spoke on the phone?"

"I... uh, wasn't picturing *anything*."

She laughs in a pleasant manner and takes Jon's arm. "I'm just kidding. C'mon, let's go inside and talk."

A surge of warmth sweeps over Jon, as the outgoing woman grips his arm and ushers him through the front gate. After a brief smile at the security guard who lets them pass, they enter the park and walk the pathway to a stone tunnel leading into the ruins. Following after her, Jon ducks inside. "Did that guard know you?"

"Everyone knows me here." They exit the tunnel to an awesome view of the ancient city. Jon scans the local remains of Mayan architecture and then turns to her. "Why?"

"Why what...?"

"Why does everyone know you?"

She turns from the ruins to smile at Jon. "I'm an anthropologist specializing in Mayan history."

"Wow... Really?"

"I've been here so many times on research trips or with university groups that they know me and just let me pass by."

Jon can't help but be charmed by her bright personality. "Having a beautiful smile probably helps."

She looks at him warmly. "Thank you. So sweet of you to say..."

Blushing at her demure response, Jon turns to look out over the abandoned Mayan city. "This is really amazing..." Rebecca takes his arm again and leads him down the footpath. Her soft voice and gentle touch put him at ease as he walks in step with her, listening to the local history.

"The ruins at Tulum are different from other Mayan cities of the Yucatan. It is the only one built on the coast, and it is unique in that it has a wall surrounding it for protection."

Jon looks around in wonder. "I've seen photos before, but being here is something else..."

"You've probably seen photographs of Chichen Itza. One of the largest in the Yucatan that has been uncovered..."

Coba Libre

Jon gazes at one of the taller ruins, hesitates, then asks, "What is inside these pyramids?"

"The Mayans were not the same builders as Egyptians. In Egypt, their pyramids were tombs constructed for burial. The Mayans used theirs to celebrate the levels of life on earth. A seed goes into the ground to grow, and as it sprouts it reaches up to the sky. These mounds are piled so they could get closer to the sky to honor the heavens."

Enamored with this fascinating woman, Jon continues to walk with her. "I hate to interrupt the excellent history lesson, but why are we here?"

She leads them away from a group of tourists and speaks in a low voice. "Julio is an interesting case, and I believe him to be a mostly honest man."

Jon nods his agreement and matches her lowered tone. "But, what about Rollie?"

"I don't know the details, but if Julio had you contact me, then I am to keep you safe until we find out more."

"Safe from what?"

She looks at him earnestly. "Dangerous circumstances."

"Like what?"

"Abduction and ransom, for instance…"

"You think Rollie was taken for ransom?"

"It looks that way."

Shocked, Jon stops whispering. "*Why?!?*"

She hushes him, as she leads him further along. "Probably hijacked for his airplane and piloting skills…"

"There must be other skilled pilots around."

Rebecca scans the area while keeping her voice down. "When I say that Julio is a mostly honest man, I mean that he is trustworthy. But, *some* of his associates are not so much…"

"How do we *know* Rollie was hijacked? Who took him, and how do we get him back?"

Leading down the path, she speaks while pretending to point out items along the tour. "Last night, a well-known smuggler's watercraft exploded not far off the Yucatan coast. There have been problems with the cartel lately, and this is probably connected."

"What were they smuggling?"

She shrugs indifferently. "Doesn't matter. If the cartels suspect it's cutting into their business, heads are going to roll."

"Is Julio involved with the cartel?"

"Not the big one in Mexico City… More of a local, junior cartel that wants to use his beach resort as an unloading point. I imagine that shipment was supposed to come through somewhere nearby last night."

Upon hearing this, Jon thinks back on the events of the previous night. Obvious clues start to make sense, including the early morning arrival of the thugs.

"We did see something like an explosion on the water last night… There was a phone call for Julio, and then Rollie was eager to leave."

Rebecca nods and keeps them moving. "I do love Julio, but sometimes he doesn't know when to stop and play it safe. He is always trying to push the envelope."

"So, some small-time thugs kidnapped Rollie?"

Coba Libre

"I don't think so. Most likely it was the big cartel that thought he was a cog in the local smuggling operation."

Jon feels a sick turn in his stomach. Suddenly paranoid, he looks around the ruins to see if people are watching them. "Do you think they'll *kill* him?!?"

She shakes her head. "Not if they want to use him to trade for the smuggled merchandise…"

"Drugs…?"

"No… Artifacts…"

Jon opens his backpack and pulls out the Mayan dagger. "Like *this*…?"

Rebecca pushes the ceremonial knife down and has him tuck it back inside his bag. "Don't wave that around in here! What are you doing with it?"

Jon shrugs and closes his pack. "I thought I might need something to protect myself with."

She rolls her eyes. "First off, that's a priceless antiquity and, secondly, if that's what it comes down to for protecting us, then we are already in *way* too much trouble."

Holding his bag, he finds a place to sit, and looks at her. "With you being an anthropologist, what do you think about Julio smuggling this stuff?"

She sits beside him and glances around at the crowds. "It is a mixed blessing. I get first dibs on studying items that I would never get my hands on otherwise, and the money supports protecting the more valuable items."

"How is that?"

"Julio is very generous, when it comes to protecting the rich history of the Mayan culture."

"By smuggling artifacts…?"

"Nobody is perfect."

Gazing at the beautiful woman sitting beside him, Jon can't help but imagine her in Julio's photo album of cenotes. "Have you known Julio a long time?"

"All my life…"

Feeling a tinge of jealousy, he looks out at the cliff-side ocean view. "What now?"

"You don't appear to have been followed. We can go to my place and wait for instructions."

"Do you know where he took Rollie's seaplane?"

"No. When he stashes something, it will be safe."

Jon looks around the ruin site and back to her again. "Was that your address he gave me?"

"No, it's a little coffee shop down the way that we sometimes meet at. I wasn't sure how you were to get there, so I picked this location, which is closer for you."

"I borrowed Julio's truck."

Her face brightens with a smile. "He loves that thing, and no one under fifty years old knows how to drive it."

"My very first car was a stick shift."

"You don't look that old."

Jon smiles back. "I'm not."

"Let's go. We can put my bike in the truck and wait for him to find us in Akumal." As they get up to leave, Jon senses that someone is watching them. He turns to see a group of tourists and notices that one of them snaps a photo in their direction. When the

Coba Libre

photographer continues to take pictures of the surrounding ruins, Jon shrugs it off as a mere coincidence and walks away with Rebecca.

XVII

Jon stands where he left Julio's truck and stares at the empty parking spot. In the next space sits a big, white passenger van. He walks around the van and, in disbelief, scans his gaze over the now-crowded parking lot. He points down at drips of oil on the cracked pavement. "Where did it go? I parked it here…"

"It's not here now."

Befuddled, he turns and stares at her. "I can see that… Why would it get towed?"

Taking his arm, she leads him away. "Julio probably came and took it."

Digging into his pocket, Jon takes out the single key. "But… I have the key."

"I doubt that's the only one he has."

Jon looks at the empty spot again. Unable to get over the missing truck, he asks, "How would he know where it was?"

Coba Libre

She checks the street and the gathering crowd of tourists. "Julio finds out stuff that you don't even want to know about. He was maybe here, but he's gone now." With Jon in tow, Rebecca heads to a rack filled with bicycles.

Still not believing that the truck is actually gone, Jon looks back and mutters, "Why didn't he come get us?"

"I don't know, but we should go. We'll take mine."

Shoulders drooping, Jon lets out a sigh as he looks to the lineup of bikes. "Not *another* bicycle ride…" They move past the bike rack and stop before a row of small motorbikes. Rebecca lifts a flaming pink helmet from the seat of one of them and hands it to Jon.

"Here… Put this on."

Jon stares at it in disbelief. *"What?!?"*

"You don't want to crack your melon, do you?"

"I don't want to ride that thing *at all!*"

"Don't be a wuss." He looks confused, and she smiles. "Yes, *I do speak-a da Americana.* I went to college in Arizona." Jon puts on the flashy helmet, while Rebecca straddles the motorbike, scoots it back from the lineup and kickstarts the engine. She grins at him and revs the throttle to warm it up. "Get on, sweet-thing. You can ride bitch." He just stands there, so she points to the spot behind her. *"Get on the back, big boy!"* When Jon clutches his backpack and reluctantly gets on, she turns to look at him. "All set?"

"Not really…"

"Hold on around my waist."

He loops his arms through the straps of his pack, pinning it to his chest, and warily puts his arms around. Getting situated, she scoots her bottom back and then looks at him accusingly. "What is that poking me in the back?"

Jon looks at his bag in front and shifts it to his back. "Sorry... It must have been the handle of that Mayan dagger." She gives him a sultry look, shimmies her backside into his crotch and laughs. "Yeah, sure it was..." Twisting the throttle on the grip, Rebecca guns the engine, releases the clutch and zooms off with them riding double.

~*~

The motorbike arrives at a cinderblock and stucco constructed apartment building. They turn into the driveway, ride to the back and stop in front of a row of garage doors. Releasing his hold from her waist, Jon slides off the bike. Rebecca kicks down the stand, shuts off the engine, and turns to see Jon trying to take his helmet off.

Laughing, she reaches over to help him with the strap. "Well, we made it here alive."

Eyeing her suspiciously, he lifts his chin to give her better access. "Uh, why do you say that as if you're surprised?" She unfastens the buckle and then steps off the motorbike. Pulling the helmet off, Jon watches her head to a back stairway, and she waves for him to follow.

Inside Rebecca's apartment, Jon looks around, amazed. The distinct Mayan décor is akin to Julio's office but displayed in a much more organized way. They pass through the kitchen, and she opens the fridge to look inside. "Would you like something to drink?"

"Anything cold is fine." She takes out two bottles of beer and hands one to Jon. He eyes the turtle label, then watches Rebecca go to the other room, sit down, and put her feet up. "What do we do now?"

She props the beer bottle on top of her knee and shrugs. "All we can do is wait."

Jon follows her into the living room and sits on the sofa. "I can't believe this is happening."

"Worrying about it a lot won't help anything. Julio will do whatever it takes to get Rollie back safe."

"I hope so…"

She takes a drink from the cold bottle and studies Jon. "So, you live in Key West?"

"Yeah… I do now, I guess."

"You don't sound very sure."

"It happened recent."

"What do you do for work?"

Jon swallows a gulp of beer. "I'm a writer."

"What kind…?"

"Books."

Rebecca's eyes twinkle and she laughs. "What *kind…?* Comic books, cookbooks, travel books…?"

"Mostly adventure-fiction…."

She nods toward the loaded bookcase across from them. "I also write, but mostly about the Mayan civilization. I guess there is a good bit of fiction mixed in there. To fill in the gaps… That's why history keeps changing."

Eric H. Heisner

After another sip of beer, Jon sets the bottle on a table and lays his head back. "I've been living way too much non-fiction these past few weeks and haven't had a lot of time for the writing I want to be doing." Suddenly feeling very fatigued, he closes his eyes and senses her move next to him on the sofa. He turns his head to look at her, rubs his eyes, and smiles. "Lately, I don't know if I'm awake or dreaming."

She reaches over and smooths her fingertips over his head to loosen-up the hair matted from wearing the helmet. "I'll wake you up for the good part."

"I appreciate you taking me in."

"That's okay… You seem like a nice-enough fella."

With his tired grin lingering, Jon lets his eyes close again. He enjoys the light touch of her sweeping back his hair and caressing his forehead. "Thank you, Rebecca…" In a moment, his eyelids relax, his breathing becomes slow and deep, and he's sound asleep.

XVIII

The phone rings, jarring Jon from sleep. He opens his eyes, looks around and realizes that he is still in Rebecca's apartment. His beer sits on the table, but she is nowhere in sight. Sitting up, he looks at the ringing telephone and finally reaches over to answer it. "Hello...?"

An old familiar voice sends chills up Jon's spine. "Johnny-boy, what the hell are you doing in Mexico?"

"Moselly?

"The one and only..."

"How did you find me here?"

"I'm your agent. It's my job."

Jon blinks his eyes and looks around the room for Rebecca again. "Did you read the new book?"

"Yes, I did, buddy. That's what I wanted to talk to you about."

"Yeah?"

"Are you playing a joke on me?"

"What…?"

"I can't sell this… There's not even a tiny hint of action, adventure, romance or mystery."

As a wave of dread sweeps over Jon, he sputters out, "It's a character-study drama."

"It's a *turd*."

"Really?"

"No marketability whatsoever…"

"You don't think it will sell?"

"I'm not in the turd-herding business."

"Wow, tell me what you *really* think…"

The obnoxious voice echoes in Jon's ears, "It's *shit!!!* That's what I *think*, Jon. Jon…"

Suddenly, Jon hears his name, as he is shaken awake. "Jon…?" He opens his eyes to see Rebecca over him with the phone cradled on her shoulder. "Julio just called. I was going to let you sleep a while longer, but you started babbling like you were having a nightmare."

Groggy, he looks at the telephone and asks, "Is it for me?"

Amused, she smiles at him and hangs up the receiver. "Are you taking calls from my place now?"

Slowly waking, Jon blinks his eyes a few more times and takes a deep breath. "Sorry… It was something from that bad dream, I guess." He reaches over for his beer, takes a swig and quickly notices that it has gone warm. He glances at the bottle, then looks outside to the dark, evening sky. "What time is it?"

"You must have been tired."

Jon sits up and sets the bottle down. "Yeah, late night…"

"Until now, not much has happened."

"Any word from Rollie?"

"In an hour, Julio is coming by to pick us up."

"What about Rollie?"

"Nothing yet, but Julio says he has a plan."

Jon rubs his eyes again, as the fog of sleep finally lifts. Rebecca steps away toward the hall and takes her shirt off to reveal a black sports-top beneath. She turns to see him staring. "I'm going to take a shower. You need one…?"

Dazed, he gawks at her. "Uh, I guess so..."

She comically remarks, "Hey, slow down there Skippy, not *with* me… You might still be dreaming."

Embarrassed, Jon quickly turns his gaze away from her. "Yeah, I know. Just waking up…"

Giggling playfully, she tosses her shirt at him and makes her way down the hallway. "Don't worry! I was only kidding… You need to lighten up."

Watching her walk away, Jon feels flush with emotions. He shakes it off and calls to her, as she steps into the bedroom. "Do you mind if I make a collect call to the States?"

"Nope… Go ahead…"

"Thanks."

Down the hall, Rebecca's bedroom door remains partly open as she undresses. She covers herself and peeks through the doorway toward her guest. "I'll be done in a few minutes, and I'll leave a towel out for you."

Jon takes a head-clearing breath and reaches over to grab the phone from the side table. He dials and waits for the operator to answer. "Yes... Hello, uh, hola... Hable Ingles? Collect call to the United States, please."

When the voice on the other end of the line acknowledges, Jon taps in the number and states his full name. There is a pulsing dial tone, until someone finally answers, "Hello, C. Moselly Literary Agency."

"Yes, is Moselly there?"

"He is in a meeting at the moment. May I take down a message from you?" Jon thinks a moment and shakes his head. "No message, thanks. Just tell him, I called."

"Hold please, I think I have a message for you." Hearing a door creak, Jon looks up to see Rebecca slip across to the bathroom. He catches a glimpse of her barely covered nakedness and looks away. The receptionist returns to the call. "Yes, Mister Moselly says for you to call him asap."

"I'm calling him right now."

"Sorry, but he is in a meeting."

Confused, Jon momentarily pulls the phone away from his ear and looks at it. "Just tell him I'll call him later."

"Is that your message?"

"Yes."

"Okay, Mister Springer. Have a nice day."

The call ends, and Jon hangs up the receiver. He hears water from the shower and sighs dreamily. Taking his warm beer from the table, he has another swallow.

~*~

Coba Libre

Outside the apartment building, Julio's truck rumbles at an idle, while a cloud of heavy exhaust lingers in the headlights. Jon and Rebecca exit the building together and walk over. Excited, Julio reaches across the cab and pushes the passenger door, which opens with a loud creak. "C'mon, the both of you! We got to go on the quick!"

Getting into the truck first, Rebecca slides to the middle. She gives Julio a friendly kiss. "We're all set."

"Thanks sweetheart."

Tossing his bag in the back, Jon notices a tarp partly covering a bunch of gear that includes scuba-diving equipment. He climbs in, pulls the door closed and looks to the driver. "We're all set for what?"

Leaning forward to see past Rebecca, Julio smiles at Jon. "I found out where they are keeping Rollie." The truck lunges ahead. "They offered a trade of goods, and he is free to go."

"Is that what you have in the back?"

"No... That is something else to work our advantage. The goal is to get Rollie back safe."

"Where is he?"

"Coba."

"What's *Coba*?"

Rebecca chimes in. "Coba is a place."

Jon looks out the cracked windshield to as far as the headlights will reach and asks, "What kind of a place is it?"

Rebecca answers, "Another ancient city of Mayan ruins, further into the jungle, not far from here..."

Puzzled, Jon turns to stare at them. "Tell me, why are we driving to some ancient city, deep in the jungle, in the middle of the night, to complete a ransom trade?"

In return, Julio shrugs. "How is it usually done?" Acquiescing, Jon thinks back on his most recent adventures. Julio shifts through the truck's gears and punches the gas pedal. "I am so very sorry to get you and Rollie involved in all this, but that is the way it goes sometimes."

Leaning forward, Jon peers past Rebecca to glare at Julio. "What was in the smuggled cargo that exploded out at sea?"

Breaking focus from his driving, Julio glances at Rebecca and then to Jon. "Less you know of details, the safer you are."

Bluntly, Jon asks, "Drugs?"

"No, no… I do not deal in such things… Anymore…"

"Artifacts?"

Curious, Rebecca sits back, arms folded, and listens to Julio's explanation. He glances at her briefly before responding. "Nothing from the Yucatan… There was a shipment of some very valuable items that I was to facilitate the importation of. Specific items of interest…"

Jon shakes his head. "Why would they blow up a boat that held valuables, and not just commandeer it?"

With both hands on the steering wheel, Julio stares ahead. "Unbeknownst to me, there might have been other items aboard that certain parties did not want to make to market."

Jon stares at Julio accusingly. "Like *drugs…?*"

"Possibly…"

Rebecca gives an unhappy grunt, and Jon looks outside to the jungle flashing by as they drive down the rural road. "What are you supposed to trade them for Rollie?"

"It is much better if you don't know such things."

"Why do you need *us* along for this?"

Unable to keep quiet any longer, Rebecca turns to Julio and bursts out with, "*What are you trading them, Julio?!?*"

A pause lingers in the conversation, until Julio looks over at them and shrugs. "It is difficult to explain."

Rebecca puts on a stern tone. "What is it *this* time?"

"Me…"

Dumbfounded, Jon and Rebecca both stare at him. Rebecca breaks the silence, uttering, "*What?!?*"

Jon asks, uncertainly, "*You…?*"

"Yes, myself… And, a certain book…"

XIX

Julio's truck travels deeper into the Mexican jungle. Illumination from the headlights shine on road signs for the ruins at Coba. Eventually, the truck slows and Julio downshifts to make a sharp turn onto a narrow, overgrown roadway. Creeping along the jungle road for several minutes, they ultimately arrive at a wide clearing in the trees where the sky breaks through. Coming to a stop, the headlights shine a beam of light over a body of water that appears to be a small lake.

The lights blink off, and Julio opens his door to get out. Jon looks at Rebecca. "What are we doing here?" She doesn't answer and shifts across the seat to get out on the driver's side. Jon sits in the darkness for a moment. Then, with a loud creak, he pushes his door open.

Coba Libre

At the back of the truck, Julio pulls the tarp off the diving equipment. He shines a flashlight on the collection of swim gear and air tanks, before he looks up to Rebecca and Jon. "We are putting into effect my insurance plan." They watch curiously, as Julio opens the tailgate and starts to unload the gear.

Not recognizing any hint of a plan, Jon naively asks, "We're going scuba-diving?"

Rebecca looks over at the dark cenote and back to Julio. "Why are there only two tanks?"

From amongst the pile of gear, Julio pulls out a waterproof sack and unrolls the top flap. "Only the two of you will be entering the ruins by the cenote."

In disbelief, Jon stares at Julio. *"We're swimming in an underground river to the ruins?"*

The white flash of a grin appears on Julio's features. "Sí... It will be safest for you both that way."

"Why?!?"

"Because it would look very suspicious to show up at a secret meeting place and have two people with me, when it was arranged for me to be all alone."

Uneasy with the proposed plan, Jon turns to Rebecca. "Have you *done* this before?"

"Exchange a hostage?"

"No! Swum this river to the ruins...!"

She nods. "Yes, I have led a few tours."

"At *night...?*"

"No, but it is dark underground, so it doesn't matter."

Jon looks back at Julio. "So, let me get this straight..." He glances at Rebecca, gets no support, and looks again to Julio. "You drive into the ruins by yourself to make the trade?"

"Yes."

"And, we swim in through the underground river?"

Julio puts an extra mask and snorkel into the waterproof bag and looks at Jon. "Sí… That's it, more or less…"

"Why?"

"Why what?"

"Why are we swimming into the ruins?"

Julio leans over the truck bed and unbuckles the lid on a steel box. He opens it, reaches inside, and brings out an object wrapped in waxed paper. "You will bring this along with you, in case things go sideways."

Jon peers at it. "What is that? It looks like a book."

"It *is* a book." Julio carefully unwraps a layer of paper to reveal a leather-bound manuscript.

Jon asks, "What's special about this book?"

The flashlight clicks on, and Julio illuminates the faint text on the cover. "This was a book written by the greatest explorers of the Yucatan."

"Who? Christopher Columbus?"

Julio exclaims, "No! That's the product of an education in the Estados Unitos… They are John Lloyd Stephens and Frederick Catherwood."

"Who are they?"

"Famous explorers."

"Never heard of them."

Coba Libre

Julio glances at Rebecca, who politely remains quiet. "Señor, in the early 1800s, they explored much of the Yucatan, as well as Copan. They discovered many sites we study today, including Tikal."

The lost look on Jon's face is too much for Rebecca, and she chimes in. "Much of what we know about the Mayan cities today comes from these two."

Utterly agape, Jon stares at them both. "I don't get it. They blew up a boat and kidnapped Rollie for an old book?"

Clicking the light off, Julio tilts his head. "Sort of."

Jon's eyes slowly adjust back to the darkness, and he asks, "How much is it worth?"

Julio glances at Rebecca again and then softly mutters, "A few hundred to some, and priceless to others…"

"Julio, are you talking pesos or dollars for this thing? Thousands…? Maybe *millions?!?*" When Jon turns to Rebecca, she shrugs, so he asks, "It's not about the *book*, is it?"

She responds unenthusiastically. "Dealing with Julio, sometimes it's better not to ask…"

They watch Julio cover the book in another wax-cloth wrapper and tuck it into a plastic bag before placing it in the waterproof sack. As he seals it closed, he looks at them both. "This book is valuable, but the information scribbled inside, along the margins, is what they want."

"And, what information is that?"

"Notes from Stephens himself on what they discovered but didn't publish in the first edition..."

Jon looks at Rebecca for a moment, and then back to Julio. "What would he choose not to include?"

Speaking in a low tone, as if to keep the surrounding jungle from hearing, Rebecca moves closer to them. "If you were to find something important and didn't want the whole world to rush in and steal it away, what would you do?"

"I wouldn't tell anyone."

She whispers, "Yes..."

"Mayan treasure?"

She looks skeptical. "Possibly... Just legends..."

Julio sets the bag on the ground next to the dive gear. "No, Rebecca, not just mere legends... Fortunes and riches not even the Spaniards could imagine...! They conquered Mexico, not for the land, but for the wealth to fund their vast empire. There is much yet to be found, and these explorers from long ago had the time, knowledge and patience to look for it."

Rebecca shakes her head. "Julio, you know that these stories are just treasure tales."

He stares at her briefly, then moves back to the truck. "My dear, *you* should know better than most that they are real."

Jon, looking at the diving gear, stands between them. "What about Rollie?"

The tailgate fastens closed with a quiet clunk, and Julio moves around to the driver's door. "I will be at the exchange. You will make the drop, we will get Rollie, and all will be well." He gets in the truck, glances at the time and looks at Rebecca. "The book must be placed under the ring on the south court by sun-up, which will be approximately six fifty-five."

He smiles at Jon, starts the truck and waves to Rebecca. "Stick to our strategy, darling, and all will be well."

Jon stares, dumbfounded, as she waves back at him. "What strategy...?" With a cloud of exhaust, the truck turns around and rumbles off in the night. Jon turns to face Rebecca. "I wasn't informed of any actual strategy."

"You were asleep."

"In the apartment...?"

"Yes."

"How long were you actually on the phone with him?"

In the moonlight, he can discern Rebecca's grimace. "Long enough for Julio to hatch this half-assed plan..."

XX

At the water's edge, Jon and Rebecca are geared up and ready to descend into the cenote. As he adjusts the shoulder straps on his air tank, he watches her stuff his backpack and all their clothing into a large dry-bag. "Sure seems like a lot of stuff... Should we leave things here, so we don't have to lug it along?"

"I don't know if we will be coming back this way again, so it's better to have it all with us."

Jon looks at the other waterproof sack containing the extra mask, snorkel and book. "Are these bags going to work?"

"If we squeeze most of the air out, they should be fine. We'll be near the surface, until we go through the underwater passages between caverns." They both look out to the star-lit sky over the dark waters of the cenote.

Flashing a broad smile, Rebecca gets ready to test the breathing apparatus on her tank. "Ready for this, Jon?"

"As ready as I'm going to be…"

"Okay… You take the book, and I'll hold onto the bag with our stuff." She wraps her lips around the mouthpiece, takes a few practice breaths and then gives Jon the thumbs up. Her eyes blink at him, as Jon tests his regulator and returns the gesture. Lugging the bigger of the two bags, she slides down the grassy embankment and eases into the freshwater pool. Following, he totes the dry sack with the book, using it as a buoy as they get into deep water.

As water laps his chest, Jon peers across the dark surface. "Anything I should worry about? Piranhas…? Sharks…?"

Rebecca lowers into the water and starts to swim, keeping her head above the surface. "This is freshwater here, unless we get closer to the ocean. There are crocs, sometimes…" With no further explanation, Rebecca puts in her breathing apparatus, lowers her face mask and sinks down.

Jon stares wide-eyed, as she recedes into the cool water. "Crocs? Do you mean *crocodiles?!?*"

Beneath the surface, Rebecca's flashlight clicks on, creating a murky underwater glow. Quickly scanning around for anything ready to eat them, Jon murmurs, "Aww, shit…" After taking a slow, calming breath, he inserts his mouthpiece, lowers his mask, and slips into the depths. His flashlight clicks on, and he swims, following Rebecca.

~*~

Coba Libre

Their flashlights lighting the way, Jon and Rebecca swim side by side only a few feet beneath the surface. As they come upon a rock wall, Jon follows her down to where a swift current flows through an opening. Using the beam of his flashlight to illuminate the dark water around them, he watches as a frog and two tiny fish float past. He shines the light toward Rebecca, just as she is about to swim into the passageway.

Suddenly, she pulls back from the opening and motions for Jon to keep back. Her beam of light illuminates a row of protruding teeth on the elongated snout of a swamp crocodile. The prehistoric-looking beast, with dark eyes that shimmer in the light, casually swims past them.

Jon freezes, trying not to panic, and drifts upward. Once the crocodile has passed, Rebecca glances up at Jon, gives an okay gesture, and motions for him to come along. Calming his breathing, he watches her swim into the cave. After a moment, the view of her light dims and finally fades. He swims down, shines his light inside and then looks behind to see only water. Hesitantly, he follows into the opening.

~*~

Surfacing in the dark, Rebecca lets the air regulator drop from her mouth, breathes, and then pushes her mask up. Jon pops up next to her and does the same. Wide-eyed, he gasps, *"What the hell was that?!?"*

"That was about an eight-footer."

"You're not kidding... It looked like twenty!"

Rebecca smiles playfully and starts to swim toward the edge of the rocky pool. "Down in the water, they don't think of us as a source of food. They're fine…"

After checking the water behind, he swims after her. "That row of teeth says different…"

"In the mangroves, or along the shoreline, is where they hunt for frogs and fish. That's where you watch out for them." She laughs. "I haven't heard of *any* cases of them having a taste for gringo tourists."

Rebecca climbs onto a rock ledge, as Jon flashes his light back into the water before quickly scrambling out. He catches his breath and smiles. "I was more worried about *you*."

Seated on the rocks above the pool, Rebecca starts to take off her gear. "Yeah… *Sure,* you were."

Jon scans around the pool with his light. "Are we here?"

To lower the bright beam, she puts her hand on his. "We're close … We should keep the flashlights off and be quiet, in case anyone is nearby."

Jon looks at the time on his wristwatch and whispers, "We still have about an hour until sunrise."

"That's fine. It's about a fifteen-minute hike through the jungle to the ruins." She unrolls the top of the waterproof bag and pulls out Jon's pack, along with her small bundle of clothes. She hands him his stuff and whispers, "Put on something dry, so you don't get swamp-ass."

As he slides his air tank straps off, Jon catches Rebecca in the moonlight, slipping out of her swim bottoms to dry off. Looking away, he mutters, "Do we leave the scuba gear here?"

"Yes, we're near enough to the tourist center and, later, Julio can send someone to pick everything up." Jon can faintly make out her half-dressed figure, as she stands beside him in the dim light. She flashes a grin in his direction and remarks, "See something you like?"

Embarrassed, Jon lowers his gaze and looks away. "Sorry… It's so dark, I can't see a thing."

After drying herself, Rebecca tosses Jon her diving mask and snorkel. "We'll put our masks in the dry bag with the book, in case we have to stash it and swim out."

He pulls a sky-blue shirt from his pack and turns to her, as she pulls on a pair of dark shorts. As he puts it on, he can sense her looking him over. He asks, "What's the matter?"

"Did you happen to have a darker colored shirt?"

Dismayed, Jon looks down to see that his shirt nearly glows in the dark. "I wasn't told to pack for a night raid."

Rebecca shrugs, pulls a dark chemise over her swim top and waves him along. "No matter… It will be light soon."

XXI

Emerging from the jungle, Jon and Rebecca come upon the Mayan ruins of Coba. Stacks of strategically placed stones form primitive altars and great pyramids built to honor the native gods in the sky. In the dawn light, Jon stands, awestruck. Rebecca takes hold of his hand and keeps him moving. "C'mon... Julio said that, by sunup, we need to put the book under the stone ring in the west ball court."

Being pulled along, Jon takes in the ancient city and asks, "Is this the game court where the losing team gets killed?"

"Not always... But, if the game was to settle a feud between villages, sometimes the losers were sacrificed."

In the growing light, he holds tight to her hand, as he studies her shapely figure moving swiftly along.

Coba Libre

She leads Jon down a path between uncovered ruins, until they are near the ball court. Rebecca suddenly pulls him aside to duck into a stacked-stone tunnel that conceals them from view. The scent of the cave's dampness fills Jon's nostrils, and he looks at her. "What now?"

To be able to see the time on his watch, Rebecca turns Jon's wrist toward the outside light. Then, she looks to the morning sky. "We'll wait for Julio to make his appearance."

"Then what?"

"The exchange happens…"

Tucked close to Rebecca, Jon feels both amorous affection and a looming sense of danger. Overwhelmed by his feelings, he murmurs under his breath. "Do you love Julio?"

Surprised by the question, Rebecca smiles and nods. "Yes, why do you ask?" She inadvertently touches Jon's arm and a tingle of excitement washes over him.

"I was just wondering if I had a chance…"

"With what?"

Her bright eyes stare directly into his, and he stutters, "Uh, well… With romance, I guess…"

The look on her face turns from surprise to confusion. She leans closer, her breath tickling his neck, and whispers, "Are you in love with Julio?"

Now, Jon is the surprised one. He responds delicately. "Uh, no… I meant with you, not him."

She continues to lean in toward him and, moving her head over just a little, her lips touch his. It takes him a moment to realize what has happened, and then he kisses her back. After a brief romantic exchange, she pulls away and rests her hand on his. "How was that for an answer?"

"Good..." He catches his breath, peers outside and mutters, "I just wasn't sure if you had a page in his book."

The whites of her eyes widen, and she replies sternly, "Are you talking about Julio's cenote book?"

Jon nods, and she slaps his hand instead of caressing it. "That's gross... Why do you say that?"

"I just figured all the girls he knew were in there."

"I'm his *cousin!*"

Relieved, Jon gasps, "You *are?*"

"Yes... What did you think?"

"You said that you loved him."

"Jon, our mothers are sisters, and we grew up together. Of course, I do." As Jon falters for words, Rebecca leans in and kisses him again. This time the kiss is more passionate, but is disrupted by the sound of approaching footsteps and voices. Her whisper raises gooseflesh on his neck. "They're coming! Stay quiet..." Jon feels the warmth of Rebecca's body next to him, as he pulls back into the chamber and moves closer to her. He looks at his watch to see that it is almost time.

They peer out into the dim morning light, as three gun-toting thugs approach the ball court. The two in front, wearing track suits, are familiar from the other day, and the larger one in back carries a bundle the size of a body over his shoulder. Trying to identify whether the limp form is dead or alive, Jon gasps, *"Is that Rollie?"*

Coba Libre

Rebecca pulls him back. "Shhh…"

They watch as the three walk down the center aisle of the ball court and stop below the cement ring at the middle. Guns held ready, the two look both ways. Then, one of them utters a few unintelligible words to the man carrying the load. Unceremoniously, the large bundle is flopped onto the ledge against the steep wall under the ring. Bound tight at the hands, arms, and feet, the body rolls over, stares skyward, heaves a few short breaths and then lies still. The men stand waiting, while one of them pulls out a gold watch from his pocket and looks at the time. Another one takes out a pack of cigarettes, which they pass around before lighting up.

Huddled close to Rebecca, Jon whispers to her, "We were supposed to leave the book under the ring."

"It's too late now. Let's wait and see." As they watch, another figure steps into the court from the opposite end.

Entering the ball court, Julio confidently advances toward the men. Not looking at the bound body, he keeps his focus on the three men with guns. Noticing Julio, one of them calls out. "Hey… Stop right there!" Tossing away his cigarette, he puts his hand to the receiver of his machine gun and waits for Julio to stop. "Where's the package?"

Julio lifts his empty hands and puts on a friendly face. "It will be arriving soon."

The group of men ready their automatic weapons, as they look around for somebody else. Next to Rollie, the big one, with a cigarette dangling from his lips, continues to smoke. Keeping close to the others, the spokesman grumbles at Julio, *"You* were supposed to bring it. *Alone…"*

"Yes."

"Yes…?"

"Before I give you what you want, I have to verify that the hostage is still alive and will be able to walk out of here." When the leader uses the barrel of his gun to motion to the big guy behind him, the thug grabs Rollie roughly by the wrist ties. He sits the seaplane pilot upright and turns him to face Julio. The morning light is not yet bright enough to see his features, so Julio calls out, "You okay, buddy?"

His mouth gagged, Rollie shrugs and nods slightly. Turning back to Julio, the main thug points his gun at him. "What about that book?"

"First, untie him."

The thug turns and nods to his henchman. Cigarette still dangling from his lips, the big guy opens a knife blade and, with a single swipe, cuts the ties on Rollie's wrists. Reaching up, Rollie removes the cloth gag from his mouth and mutters, "Thanks, pal…" He wiggles his arms free, and then starts to untie his ankles.

Impatient, the lead thug jabs the tip of his gun barrel in Julio's direction. "Let's get on with it, already. We are supposed to exchange for you *and* the book."

Julio glances to the sun rising over the east wall of the ball court and then looks directly at the stone-constructed chamber where Jon and Rebecca are still hiding. He checks the time on his wristwatch, ponders something and then nods. "Yes, it should be here in a minute."

XXII

Concealed in the alcove near to the ball court, Jon looks at Rebecca questioningly. "Is this part of the great plan?"

"I guess so. Give me the dry sack with the book."

Jon looks outside, then at the bag. "I'll take it."

"No, *I'll* do it."

"I'm not going to let you go out there."

"You don't speak Spanish."

Confounded, he replies, "So?"

"A lot could happen out there with those terrible men, and you wouldn't know what's going on." When Rebecca reaches for the dry-bag, Jon slips past her. Before she can react, he is outside, facing one of the armed men, while the others still have their back to him.

The thug lets out a soft alerting whistle to the others. They turn to see Jon, standing alone, holding the bag. The leader gestures with the tip of his gun for Jon to come closer. "Bring the bag here, Señor."

From behind them, Julio calls, "Drop it and go, please."

Jon takes a step forward and stops. He looks at the bag and demands, "Let them go, and I'll bring the bag."

Seated on the wall, Rollie finishes untying his legs and scoots a bit down the incline. The big guy turns to him, glares, and points the knife. Rollie stops, smiles and raises his hands. "Easy there, fella…"

The principal thug turns and looks from Julio to Rollie, and then back at Jon. "No, that is not how it will be, Muchacho. We exchange this man for him *with* the book."

"I am the one with the book."

"Are you a blood Mayan?"

Jon stares at the men holding guns and looks past them to see Julio creeping closer. Attempting to keep their attention, he replies, "I write books."

Amused, the leader of the group chuckles and looks to his henchmen. He keeps his gun pointed at Jon, as he casually takes out another cigarette and tosses it between his lips. "Really? Did you write *this* one, Gringo?"

"I haven't even opened it."

The thug lights his cigarette and blows a cloud of smoke. "We don't want to have to kill you for interfering." With the lit cigarette dangling from the side of his mouth, he grumbles, "Why don't you be a good American-boy and bring that bag over here."

Eric H. Heisner

Jon unrolls the top flap of the dry-bag and peeks inside. Next to the book and the masks and snorkels, sits a Colt model, semi-automatic small caliber handgun. Jon reaches into the bag.

The thug raises his gun directly at him and grunts, "Hold it there, Vato."

Jon freezes and looks up at them. Meekly, he replies, "It's just a book..."

The leader takes a long drag from his cigarette, holds it, and then puffs out smoke rings. "And, that's all it better be..." When Jon lifts the book from the bag and holds it out in front of him, the thug adds, "Bring it here, Pendejo."

Jon uses the book to motion for them to come closer. "Why don't you come over here and get it?"

"Ya me tienes harto!" Tossing the cigarette away, the leader waves his weapon to direct his associates behind him. "¡Vete a la chingada!" Jon breaks into a sweat as he realizes the situation that he has put himself into. The two men advance toward him, one with a knife and the other with a machine gun.

Trying not to panic, Jon states, "Put the guns down."

As they continue to advance, one of them flashes a smile. Their leader mockingly declares, "Why don't you put the book down and run like the wind, Senorita Gallina?"

Jon lifts the bag, drops the book inside, reaches down past it and grabs the pistol. He raises it and points it at the men, demanding, "Stop! Put down your weapons and let them go!"

Paying no heed to the warning, the two continue toward Jon as their leader laughs amused. "What will you do with that? You think you can shoot us?"

Jon looks to Rollie, who is wide-eyed in astonishment, and then again to Julio, who continues to slowly close in. Aiming the gun, Jon threatens, "I'll shoot if I have to…"

They keep advancing, and Jon points the gun skyward, jerking the trigger to let off a warning shot. Nothing happens. Pausing, the men exchange a quizzical look and start to laugh. Unimpressed, the leader takes out another unfiltered cigarette, shakes his head and quips, "You should have a child's cap gun, like the Old West cowboys in the Estados Unidos, so you will know how to use it."

Jon examines the gun and, using the hand holding the dry sack, jerks the slide back. The gun makes a cocking sound, and the advancing men halt. Jon looks up. "I've got it now!"

Flicking a flame on his lighter, the leader replies, "Have you?"

Jon aims the gun toward the tilted wall of the ball court, pulls the trigger, and the bullet skitters off the rocks. The blast gets everyone's attention. Weapons ready, the men resume their advance, until another voice calls from the sidelines. "Hold it, you guys!!!"

Everyone turns to see the attractive woman that steps from the dark passageway into the daylight. Their attentions are focused on Rebecca when, unexpectedly, the leader of the thugs orders, "Put down your guns. *Now, dammit…!*"

They all turn to see Julio behind the leader, gripping him in a chokehold and now holding his gun. The man lets the smoking cigarette tumble from his mouth and gasps, "You won't get away with this…"

"We're only looking to go away."

Jon adds, "No one has to get hurt…"

Rollie hops off the wall and, as his feet hit the ground, the big thug throws his knife at him. Reacting quickly, Julio pushes the man he is holding toward Rollie to act as a shield. With a sickening *thwack*, the blade sticks in the leader's neck. He yelps in pained anguish and falls at Rollie's feet. Unbelievably, the knife-stuck man gets on his hands and knees, crawls to his associate, and reaches up to grab the machine gun from his hands.

The shock of the moment is shattered when the man, with the blade still lodged in his neck, stands. He jerks back the bolt and pulls the trigger, letting bullets fly in every direction. Holding both the bag with the book and the small handgun, Jon dives to the side, rolls, and then races toward Rebecca.

Intermittent blasts of automatic gunfire echo through the stone ball court. Jon reaches Rebecca and tries to protect her. Instead, she grabs the small handgun from him and fires off several rounds toward the two thugs in the middle of the fray.

One of the thugs goes down, mortally wounded, and the other turns to aim the barrel of his assault rifle in their direction. When he fires, Jon hastily grabs Rebecca by the arm, pulling her to safety behind an ancient stone pillar, as bullets skitter across the rock pathway.

XXIII

As the morning light filters through a choking haze of gun-smoke, Julio pounces on the knife-struck leader and knocks the machine gun from his hands. He gets a grip on the knife handle protruding from the man's neck and jerks it free. The man screams in pain, as he attempts to stem the flow of blood gushing from the gaping hole. Without a moment's hesitation, Julio hurls the knife at the remaining thug, and the blade sticks between the man's shoulders. Merely wounded, the man turns and jerks the trigger of his weapon, only to hear an empty click. He ejects the spent ammo clip and reloads a fresh one.

Spotting another assault rifle on the ground nearby, Rollie goes for the weapon, scoops it up and quickly fires it. Three short bursts hit the mark, and the last of the thugs spins to the ground before letting off another shot. Julio watches the man slump dead against the stone wall and slide down. Impressed, he looks at Rollie and grins. "Nice shootin', Tex!"

"Thanks for the rescue, pal…"

"Just like old times."

"Yeah, hardly!"

They both see Jon and Rebecca hesitantly emerge from behind the protective stone column. Surveying the carnage, Rebecca stands holding the small handgun, while Jon holds the dry-bag tight to his chest.

Rollie slaps a fresh clip into the machine gun and addresses Jon. "I see you've met another of Julio's cousins."

Jon follows Rebecca past the two dead cartel members, and they peer down at the third guy, bleeding from his neck. The man looks up at them, tries to take out another cigarette and then dies. Jon shakes his head. "Those things will kill you." Jon looks at Julio and then to Rollie. "Glad you're not dead."

"Me, too! Thanks." The pilot smiles fondly at Rebecca. "It's been a long-time, darlin'."

"Good to see you too, Rollie."

With a tinge of jealously, Jon looks from Rollie to Rebecca and then back again. "I just found out she's a cousin."

She gives Jon a gentle pat on the back, and Julio tilts his head in confusion, as he hands one of the machine guns to Jon. "Did I say different?"

Rollie takes an ammunition clip from one of the dead men and gives it to Jon. "Here ya go, buddy. It's all we have." Jon looks down at the semi-automatic weapon and gulps. "What am I going to do with this?"

Rollie gives Julio a disapproving look and then explains to Jon, "My Mexican friend, here, has got us into the middle of a really bad situation. These guys are just the messengers. When they don't come back, others will be showing up."

Befuddled, Jon stares at them. "All this over a book?"

Julio answers calmly, "It is the knowledge between the pages that they want." He tilts his head and gestures for them to follow. Rollie starts after him, but Jon remains stationary. "Why don't they just go to a library?"

Rebecca hands Jon his backpack and ushers him along. "The explorer's notes are only found in this particular book." Jon puts on his pack, follows her, and wonders why he is the one still holding the dry-sack containing the book. He looks down at the unsightly weapon in his other hand and mutters, "I prefer it when they give me the old-fashioned gun..."

~*~

As he follows the group through the ruins, Jon passes several rock monuments devoted to the Mayan sun god. Making their way around a tablet dedicated to a tribal leader, Julio steps out and jumps back quickly. *"Damn..."*

Rollie peeks out and sees that men are gathered around Julio's truck. He makes a count and takes note of their guns. "Only three of them to our four..."

Julio shrugs. "Not *too* bad..."

"There might be more nearby." The pilot looks to Jon and Rebecca, then back at Julio. "Where's my airplane stashed? Anywhere near to here?"

"It is not close. The first thing I did when you went missing was to put it in a safe place."

Rebecca scoots forward between them and whispers, "Was that before, or after, you searched the offshore wreckage for anything salvageable?" Julio flushes with embarrassment and Rollie glares at him, knowing the predictable reality of dealing with his old friend.

Quickly regaining his composure, the Mexican offers, "And, it was a good thing I did, or we would not have had anything to bargain with for your release."

Not following, Jon asks, "I thought they wanted you along with the book?"

Julio shrugs. "They needed someone to read it."

Grimacing at Julio, Rebecca adds, "All the notes in the book are transcriptions of ancient Mayan texts."

Jon stares at her. "Can you read Mayan?"

"Yes... There are several scholars who can."

"Why don't they get one of them?"

Rebecca nods her head at her cousin and replies sternly, "Julio, here, is the only one who is, let's say... compromised in his morals enough to lead anyone into sacred ruins for the street market value of the find."

They turn to see Julio's innocent smile. "What can I say? I am a river to my people and have many sizable bills to pay." He looks at Rebecca and shakes a finger at her. "You my dear, have benefitted more than once from my findings."

Shushing him, Rollie looks at the men surrounding the truck and then ducks back. "Glad you haven't changed much, but how are we going to get clear of here?"

"We could rush them...? Try not to shoot at the truck." Julio readies his gun and makes a move around the corner only to quickly jump back. "Never mind..." The rest of them peek out to see that several overly excited men are joining the group. Their Spanish chatter can faintly be heard. Julio translates. "They heard shots, thought it was their guys and have found them in the court. They are to spread out and look for us."

Clammy with sweat, Jon inquires, "*What now...?*"

Rollie gestures toward the truck, as the cartel members start to break into groups. "I think we can still go for the truck. Wait until they split up, and then rush who's left and take it."

Looking at the automatic weapon clutched in his hands, Jon grumbles, "But, I don't even know how to use this."

Julio reaches over and slides the bolt back until it clicks and then points to the gun's receiver. "You just pull the trigger. But, not yet...Wait for us to shoot first."

Watching as several men split off, Rebecca shakes her head at the odds of successfully overcoming those that remain. "We could swim."

Julio looks at her, only partly convinced. "To where?"

"The coast..."

He shakes his head. "That's a very long way, and one wrong turn will find us lost in the middle of the jungle."

Jon looks back in the direction they came from earlier. "Would the two air tanks last us that long?"

Rebecca points at the waterproof bag that Jon still holds. "We don't need the dive tanks. We can snorkel most of it."

"But, we only have three snorkels..."

Rollie arches an eyebrow. "Fine. I'd rather fight."

Escape plans racing around in his head, Julio speaks low. "We could split up."

Jon shakes his head. "We just rescued Rollie without getting killed, and now you want us to go our separate ways and take our chances?"

Another pair of thugs split away from the truck, leaving only two of them on guard. Julio murmurs, "Back to plan A..." They all peer out to see the remaining men sharing a cigarette.

Jon whispers, "I still don't think it's a good idea."

Julio passes his machine gun to Rollie and tilts his chin. "Remember what happened in Guatemala?" Rollie's jaw drops, but before he can respond, Julio grabs Rebecca's hand and pulls her out into the open.

XXIV

Stepping out into the open, Julio drags Rebecca behind him. He calls to the two men at the truck. "Hola, amigos! Que pasa?" As she is pulled along, Rebecca briefly looks back to Jon.

Jon whispers to Rollie. "What happened in Guatemala?"

Dejectedly, the pilot lowers his gaze. "Don't ask..." Looking at the two machine guns in his hands, Rollie takes a few calming breaths.

Jon watches him, unsure what to do. "Well, do we have some sort of a plan?"

"Yeah... When I make the move, stay close behind me." He nudges the barrel of Jon's gun away and smiles feebly. "And, make sure that thing isn't pointed in my direction..."

They look out to see Julio talking with the pair of men at the truck. The Mexican waves in the direction from which he just came, and then he puts up two fingers. The two men ready their guns and approach. Jon ducks back and hisses at Rollie. *"Did he just tell them where we are?!?"*

"Get ready…"

As they move away, Julio ushers Rebecca to the truck. Suddenly, with machine guns raised and ready, Rollie steps out from around the corner to face the thugs. "Hola! Qué tal?" Dumbfounded, the two men stare at Rollie and then look back to see Julio and Rebecca at the truck. The cigarette falls from one man's mouth, and he looks down at his gun.

Rollie motions for them both to drop their weapons. "Put 'em on the ground… Easy, muchachos…." One of them unslings his weapon from his shoulder and starts to lower it, when a spray of bullets suddenly hits the wall next to Rollie. The pilot jumps back, turns and fires both machine guns in the direction of the hostile gunfire. "Jon! Get to the truck!"

Alternating bursts of gunfire from each machine gun, Rollie dashes toward the truck. As Jon runs behind, he sees Julio and Rebecca get inside. The shooting and belching roar of the truck's engine brings more men from the jungle. Another shower of bullets tears up the pathway just before Jon's feet, and he veers off his route to the truck.

Jon ducks behind a nearby stack of stones, as chips of rock shower over him. Watching Rollie go with guns blazing, Jon stays put, pinned down. When Julio shifts into gear, a cloud of exhaust pours from the tailpipe, and the truck rolls forward. Pausing at the truck, Rollie hollers, "*C'mon, Jon! Keep moving!!!*"

Releasing another short spurt of gunfire, Rollie tosses down an empty machine gun and leaps into the open truck bed. He sits up and sees that Jon, with his backpack on and the dry-bag clutched to his chest, is tucked behind the low rock wall, still trapped by opposing gunfire. As the truck accelerates to drive away, Julio glances over his shoulder to the truck bed, just as several bullets smash through the rear window. Distressed, Julio shouts to Rollie, "I'll never find a replacement window!"

The truck steers toward a road through the jungle, and Rebecca looks out the side window back to Jon, left behind. "What about *Jon?* We can't *leave* him...!"

Julio cranks the wheel. "Does he have the book?"

Rollie pops up in back and, with his remaining machine gun, opens fire at several thugs emerging from the pathways. He yells between bursts. "We have to go back for him!" Downshifting, Julio turns the steering wheel and brings the truck around. As they circle, Rollie waves for Jon to make a run for it and then ducks down, as bullets whiz over his head.

In the cab, Rebecca exchanges a look with Julio. He gapes at her in surprise, when she says, "Keep going. Don't stop..." Hovering his foot over the brake pedal, he awaits instruction. Rebecca looks out the window as they approach Jon's position. "Just slow it down enough for me to get out. We'll meet with you at the drop-off or at the ruins in Tulum." While working the clutch and gear shifter, Julio looks at her and nods. "God-speed, cousin!"

As the truck slows, the passenger-side door flies open, and Rebecca hits the ground running. Through a hail of gunfire, she dashes to Jon. Without breaking stride, she grabs his hand in passing, and pulls him along. Bullets whiz around them, crashing into the trees as the sound of the truck is heard roaring down the roadway, departing.

~*~

Sitting tucked in a stone hideaway, they huddle close, listening for the gunfire to cease. Jon notices Rebecca's calm breathing and has the sudden urge to kiss her. He abstains, deciding that it isn't the proper time or place. Giving her a squeeze, he looks around the chamber. "Thanks for saving me."

"No problem…"

"What are we supposed to do *now?*"

She puts her finger up to his lips and shushes him. Protected by the darkness of their hiding spot, she points out at two armed men at the edge of the jungle. Jon gets gooseflesh when she leans over to whisper in his ear. "At the big pyramid, there is a concealed passageway that leads down into a cenote. We can get out through there."

"We're going to try to swim all the way to the *ocean?* Julio said it was too far. *And, dangerous…!*"

"No, we'll only swim to a spot where we can get out somewhere in the jungle." Jon looks down at the dry-bag. "Why didn't we come in that way?"

Coba Libre

"It has a closed-off entrance, and a very steep climb out." He starts to speak, but she shushes him again and points to the men coming back around. The men eventually disappear into the bushes at the edge of the jungle and Rebecca turns to Jon. She gives him a peck on the cheek. "Okay, it's clear. Let's go!" Flushed with romantic desire for her, Jon is tugged along behind as she steps out of the chamber and dashes toward the largest of the pyramids.

XXV

Rebecca knows her way through the ruins, and Jon stays close behind her while weaving around columns of archaic rock carvings and stone formations. Occasionally, he looks back, expecting to see men with guns coming after them. She tugs at his hand, urging him along. "Stay close, Jon…"

Arriving at the largest of the ancient stone temples, Jon looks up in amazement. "There is a cenote under that thing?"

"Yes, this is one of the few that has an interior chamber. Most of these mounds are packed solid. There is nothing inside. They are built to reach up to the heavens."

"Not as tombs, like the Egyptian pyramids?"

"Rarely have they been found to have any chambers on the inside. They are sacrificial mounds, not burial mounds." Holding his hand, she leads him up the stone stairway in front of them. They make their way halfway to the top, where there is a wide platform. Then, they then move around to the side. They stop at a doorway piled full of rocks to block the entry. He watches her remove stones and place them aside.

From the high vantage point, he looks out at the ancient ruins of the city and stands mesmerized as the sun comes up over the trees. Finally, he sees that Rebecca has exposed a passageway leading inside. "Why was it blocked?"

"To keep tourists from falling in and drowning…"

"Drowning…?"

She places another stone aside and looks back at him. "There is a drop off to the water below."

"Have people died in there?"

She pushes a rock away from the entrance and nods. "Dozens of skeletal remains are at the bottom of this cenote."

"Tourists…?"

"We believe them to be sacrificial remains."

Jon looks toward the ruins again and spots an armed group of men heading in their direction. He gets down next to her and pulls a rock from the opening. "Can I help…?"

"Almost there..."

Jon glances to the men at the base of the pyramid and sees that someone has spotted them. "I think we can make it."

"A few more…" With the crack of a rifle, a bullet skitters off the wall. Rebecca looks down at more men coming out of the jungle to join the ones starting to climb the steps. "Okay, close enough!" She ducks inside. Jon follows close behind, wearing his backpack and holding the bag containing the book.

~*~

Making their way through the narrow passageway, Jon keeps close to Rebecca. The disturbed dust makes him cough, and he looks behind at the light streaming through the opening. He asks, "How far is it?"

"We're almost there."

Ahead, Rebecca disappears into the darkness, and Jon looks behind one more time to the glow of the sun from outside. Moving forward, he is met by the sound of her breathing and the distinct scent of moisture coming from somewhere below. He reaches his hand out and there is nothing but a black void. "Hello…? Rebecca…?"

A flashlight clicks on, and Jon sees her standing at the edge of a dark abyss. She aims the light toward his feet and puts her hand out. "Stop! Stay there…"

Jon instantly freezes and then looks down to where she shines the beam of light. The water, twenty feet below, is as clear as glass. Jon wonders aloud, "How deep is it?"

"No diving, Greg Louganis…"

Clutching the dry-bag to his chest, he scoots next to her. "Is this safe?"

After shining the flashlight around the edges of the pool, she looks at Jon and shrugs. "Probably safer than running through the jungle with those men shooting at us…" Jon stares at the crystal-clear water and sighs. Rebecca takes the dry-bag from him, opens it, and gets out the diving masks with their attached snorkels. Handing one set to him, she holds onto the other. "Loop your arm through. Don't lose it when you jump."

Jon slips his arm through the strap of his mask and hooks his thumbs on the shoulder straps of his backpack. Looking at Rebecca, he feigns a grin. "I hope we don't die."

Rebecca smiles back, leans in close and gives him a kiss. Reaching his arm out to embrace her, he suddenly stops when they hear rocks tumbling at the tunnel entrance. The patter of footsteps is followed by the crack of a gunshot. They both duck. The bullet rattles through the dark chamber, and the romantic mood is shattered.

Hurriedly, she squeezes a pocket of air from the dry-bag, rolls the top down and clips it closed. Pointing the light at the water below, she asks, "Ready for this?"

"Yeah… But who should go first?"

Not wasting any time, she gives Jon a push over the edge and jumps along with him. As the beam of the flashlight descends to the cenote, there are two simultaneous splashes. Surfacing, Jon peers around the dark cavern. He is quickly joined by Rebecca and her light. She sweeps back strands of her wet hair and smiles at him. "See…! That wasn't too hard."

Unconvinced, he adjusts his backpack on his shoulders. "Thanks for the shove."

"Put your mask on and follow me." They pull their diving masks on, and she adjusts her snorkel. "Don't stray off into any side caverns."

"Why?"

"Some of them don't surface, and you could be lost underground forever. Keep your eyes glued on my backside."

He tries to hide a grin. "That shouldn't be a problem..." Smiling at him, she wraps her lips around the mouthpiece of her snorkel and points the flashlight downward. The beam illuminates several piles of skeletal remains. Stunned, Jon's eyes open wide. She laughs, before she ducks underwater and starts to swim away. Keeping his attention focused on the glow of the flashlight and her kicking feet, he puts in his snorkel and follows.

XXVI

The morning sun shines through the thick jungle canopy surrounding the cenote just outside the city ruins of Coba. Surfacing in the tranquil pool, Rebecca lets the snorkel drop from her mouth, removes her mask and looks around for Jon. When he swims up beside her, they look at their pile of diving gear still on the shore. Jon scans their surroundings and only hears the sounds of the jungle. "They aren't here."

Rebecca climbs out of the water and studies their own footprints from earlier that morning. "Nobody comes by here. The main road is too far a hike for most."

"What now…?"

"We can hike out from here or use the diving gear to swim back to last night's drop-off point."

Sitting at the edge of the cenote, Jon looks around at the trees and the Mayan ruins beyond. The clear water looks much more inviting in daylight than it did in the dark. "We choose between crocodiles or the cartel, eh?"

Rebecca shakes her hair out. "It's up to you."

"Let's swim back to the drop-off location and hope that they are waiting for us there."

"Good choice..." She goes to the diving gear and separates hers out of the pile. "Just think... This sort of adventure is what most people come to the Yucatan for."

"I've sure had my fill of it." He stuffs his backpack, along with their other wet stuff in the larger dry-bag and seals it. "Lately, adventure is the only thing on the menu."

"It will give you some material to write about."

Jon grabs his scuba tank and checks the air supply. "Every time I'm at risk of dying, people tell me that."

She adjusts the tank on her shoulder and grabs her mask and fins. "Actually... You could die anytime. It's when you're in danger that you really feel alive."

Jon watches her take her gear to the water's edge and then put her fins on. He looks at her and then notices the light filtering through the trees. "Wow... This is an amazing place. With beautiful scenery..." She looks back at him and flashes one of her charming smiles. He grabs his stuff and walks to the water, muttering, "Too bad people out there trying to kill us."

~*~

At the drop-off point, Jon and Rebecca emerge from the clear, still water of the cenote. They climb onshore, remove their diving masks and notice the tracks left from Julio's truck the evening prior. Jon sweeps back his hair and heaves a breath. "Nobody is here, either…"

Rebecca studies the ground and then looks off toward the road. "And, there hasn't been anyone here since last night."

"Do we keep swimming, using the underground river, all the way to the coast?"

As he stands in his scuba gear, she looks down at the air-level on her tank. "We won't get far with these."

Jon looks around at the jungle and then to the roadway. "So, we walk then?"

After dropping the air tank from her shoulders, Rebecca starts to remove the rest of her unneeded gear. "Don't worry… We still have what everyone wants, so someone will find us."

Not feeling reassured, Jon scans the calm waters of the cenote behind them and then comments on the lack of traffic on the road. "Yeah… That's what bothers me."

~*~

Walking the jungle road leading away from the cenote, Rebecca carries the dry-bag with the book, and Jon carries the wet backpack on his shoulder. He steps up beside her, looks back and then looks ahead. "Won't the bad guys who are searching for us be on this road?"

"Possibly, but unless you want to bushwhack through thick jungle, this is the only road that leads to the highway."

He looks at the tangle of brush on either side of the roadway and decides that this is the best path. "And, you think Julio and Rollie will find us here?"

She smiles and shrugs. "Possibly…"

Suddenly, in the distance, they hear the sound of a truck engine shifting gears. Rebecca motions Jon to the side of the road, and they duck into the foliage as the vehicle approaches. Finally, the vintage Dodge Power Wagon, with Julio in the driver's seat, comes into view and rumbles down the roadway.

Emerging from the bushes, Rebecca slaps Jon's backside and grins happily. "See, Jon! Sometimes things *do* work out!" As the truck approaches, Jon breathes a sigh of relief and waves.

XXVII

Seated three abreast in the cab of the truck, Jon holds his wet pack on his lap and has the dry-bag tucked down by his feet. Jon looks over at Julio and, above the noise of the engine, asks, "What's the plan now?"

The driver peers over the dash, and then glances at Rebecca and Jon. "We must still give them a book."

Rebecca rolls her eyes and Jon, astounded, blurts out, "What...? *Really...?!?*"

As the truck snakes through the countryside, Julio grips the oversized steering wheel and answers, "Yes, my friend. That was the plan all along."

Rebecca, sitting between them, clenches her jaw when Jon asks, "What about the Mayan treasures?"

"In a hundred or so years, no one has found them yet. Might be another hundred...."

Jon looks to Rebecca, sensing her annoyance, and asks, "What about Rollie?"

"He will meet with us after."

"After what…?"

"The drop."

"Where is the drop location?"

"In my backyard."

Jon is confused. "At your hotel in Tulum…?"

"That wouldn't be wise. Something more public."

Rebecca grumbles, "The coastal ruins…?"

Julio turns to her and smiles. "It *is* a popular spot."

Jon complains, "Julio, I don't see how our situation has improved over the last twenty-four hours."

Rebecca makes a groaning sound, shakes her head and stares at the bullet-cracked windshield, not wanting to look at her cousin. "I don't either."

Getting the cold shoulder when he looks at Rebecca, Julio winks at Jon. "We now have the advantage!"

Surprised, Jon lifts an eyebrow. "Yeah…? How's that?"

"We have the book, and the exchange on our turf."

"So, what about you?"

Downshifting gears for a sharp turn, Julio hangs loose on the steering wheel as he drives. "I talked to some people."

Rebecca turns to look at him. "What people…?"

He smiles innocently at her and shifts up a gear, as he speeds into the straightaway. "The people who matter with these sorts of things... I let them know where I stashed some of the loot I recovered from that shipment. Several items turned out to be *very* important to them."

Skeptical, she grunts, "Now you're off the hook?"

"Let's say, I'm on retainer for my expertise in certain areas of special interest."

Jon looks at them and can't believe what he's hearing. Rebecca stares ahead again. "Shady, Julio... Very shady..."

Julio shrugs apathetically. "Many things only grow and prosper in the shade."

Clenching her jaw, Rebecca counters, "Yeah *primo*... With plenty of animal fertilizer... One of these days, things will come to light and not go well."

With both hands on the steering wheel, Julio glances at his two passengers and grins. "Laws of the jungle, cousin... Laws of the jungle..."

~*~

Driving up to the ruins at Tulum, Jon notices this time, the roadside is lined with tourist buses and street vendors. Amazed at the crowds of people walking around, Jon utters, "There are *a lot* of people here."

Julio slows the truck and taps the horn to get two men on a motorbike out of his path. "Yes, there are... *Much* safer..." He swings into a parking spot, gets out, and then looks at the gear piled in back. His gaze travels up to the bullet shattered rear window and then to Rebecca and Jon still sitting inside. "Hello...? Are you both coming along?"

Coba Libre

Surprised, Jon looks through the back window to Julio. "Shouldn't we stay here and watch the truck?"

"I doubt anyone will carry it off. It would be much safer, if you were to remain with me."

Jon swaps a skeptical look with Rebecca and mutters, "Safer for who...?"

She shrugs and glances outside at the crowds of people. "The truck will be fine."

"What about us?"

"He's probably right. Mixing in amongst the crowds of tourists might be the safest place for us."

Holding his backpack and the dry-bag, Jon swings the door open. Julio reaches over the truck bed and waves to Jon. "Toss me those bags. We will leave everything that we don't need and use your travel pack, so we don't look suspicious." Jon tosses both bags into the truck bed, and Julio grabs them.

Jon grumbles, "Do you mean stuff like that gun?"

Good-humoredly, Julio looks at him. "You must admit, the gun did come in very handy."

"It got three people killed."

"Sí, but it was on *their* side, not ours."

Looking across the parking lot to a Federales transport, Jon counts the soldiers standing around. He turns back to Julio and asks, "No more guns, I hope?"

"There is a strong military presence here, so there will be no need." Removing some wet clothing from the backpack, Julio sets it aside. He finds the Mayan ceremonial dagger, recognizes it, and looks at Jon. "Ahh, from my collection... What were you to do with this?"

"Protect myself..."

Julio smiles his approval and returns the fancy dagger to the backpack along with the valuable book wrapped in plastic. He secures the straps on the top flap and tosses the pack back across the truck to Jon. "Okay, let's go."

Jon looks at his loaded-up bag, and then back at Julio. "You want me to carry it?"

"It's your bag."

"But, it's *your* book!"

Julio glances at Rebecca and then puts on a grin for Jon. "It will look much less suspicious if you carry your own bag."

Reluctantly, Jon grabs the backpack from the truck and slings it over his arm. Beside him, Rebecca puts her hand on his shoulder. "It will be fine. Julio usually knows what he's doing."

He looks at her unsure. "I hope so…"

Following Julio, they walk to the entrance gates, where a line of tourists waits to gain access to the ruins.

XXVIII

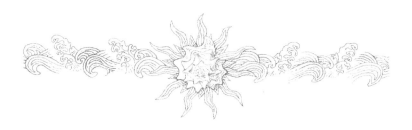

Jon, Rebecca and Julio move along with the crowds of tourists that are teeming inside the walls of the historic park. At one of the ruins, Julio pulls them aside and pretends to set them up for a couples photograph. Using the camera on his cell phone, he clicks several pictures, all the while lowly whispering to them, "Across the way, at that ruin with the double set of rooms, we're supposed to make the drop."

Jon puts on a smile for the picture, as Rebecca wraps her arms around him. He asks, "How are you supposed to do it?"

"If I make the drop myself, they might just be tempted to grab me and be done with it."

Rebecca sighs with annoyance and grimaces. "Great… So, now we know the real reason you brought us along."

Shaking his head, Jon turns away from the camera to face her. *"You're* not going to do it. I'll make the drop."

She takes her arm from around his waist and looks at him with disappointment. "Don't go all machismo on me now, Mister Adventure-writer. I can handle myself just fine."

"Uh, yes… I know you can. It's just that there is no need for you to be there."

She looks at her cousin, who continues to snap photos. "This is Julio's problem, not yours."

Julio stops with the picture-taking. "No worries. I can go myself and take my chances."

They both look at the stout little man and can't help but feel empathy for him. Clinging to the strap of the backpack on his shoulder, Jon whispers to Rebecca. "If it's only a drop off, we can do it together easy enough." He looks back to Julio. "What happens when they get what they want, and then you go back home?"

Unsure, Julio shrugs. "There are actually many different groups involved in this local power struggle. Each one trying to get the upper hand on the other… If I don't make it too easy for them to catch me unprepared, and if I play my angles right, it should be okay when things cool down."

Rebecca groans, "Always playing the angles…"

Her cousin smirks. "Is there any other way to play?"

~*~

As crowds of tourists fill the pathways between the ruins, Jon and Rebecca go to one of the roped-off buildings. They step over the barrier and make their way inside. Examining the engineering of the supportive roof timbers and the rock wall that once held a wooden door, Jon gasps, "Rebecca, these ruins are *amazing*…"

"Yes… the Mayans really were. Hundreds of years ago, a civilization was lost and then consumed by the jungle."

He witnesses her in her element and his pulse throbs. "It's been… exciting to meet you. To say the *least*."

She smiles sweetly at him and then gestures to a stone platform at the back of one of the two chambers. Heart racing, Jon studies it and opens his mouth, about to ask if it is a bed. As if reading his mind, Rebecca gives him a scolding look. "No! That's *not* for sleeping… Julio said to leave the book there."

He feigns a look of innocence, slings the pack off his shoulder and unbuckles the top flap. Suddenly, they hear a gunshot, and Rebecca rushes to look out one of the windows. As Jon reaches into his bag, she looks back and hisses at him. "*Stop…!*"

Jon freezes. "What?"

"Julio said if something goes amiss, abandon the plan and get out right away."

Pulling his hand out of the backpack, Jon looks behind and then back at Rebecca staring through the opening in the wall. "*Yeah…?!?*"

Keeping low by the windowsill, she waves him over. "Something is definitely amiss…" Another gunshot shatters the silence, and then someone's scream is followed by the sounds of people running. Rebecca looks at Jon, as he squats down. "Let's get out of here..."

Tossing the pack over his shoulder, Jon peers outside. "Where are we going to go?"

"I know this place better than anyone else. Follow me!" She takes his hand. Keeping low, she leads him out the door of the ruin, and they dash toward one of the ceremonial mounds.

At the base of the monument, Rebecca and Jon turn to see dozens of shrieking tourists fleeing the ancient city through the few exits in the surrounding walls. At the center of it all, several men, clad in colorful tracksuits and wielding machine guns, fire into the air to clear the area. Jon points to the men. "Are those Julio's pals?"

"I don't see him, so he probably cleared out."

On the opposite side of the grounds, another group of men, suited-up like Italian mobsters from the movies, appears. They begin shooting at the men in sports gear. Jon and Rebecca hunker down, as gunfire sprays across the ruins. Jon gasps, "What the heck? Who are those guys...?"

"They must be the other side of the power struggle."

He peeks out, "With us caught in the middle...!"

"And, poor Julio..."

Jon looks flabbergasted. "I think he is *far* from being an innocent bystander. I would say he's to blame for *all* of this!"

Looking at the steep stone stairs behind them, Rebecca grunts. "Yeah... Probably..." She keeps hold of

Coba Libre

Jon's hand. "That little troublemaker is always caught up in something." Leading him along, Rebecca whispers, "While they try to kill one another, let's get away from here!"

Jon points to the mass of tourists jamming the exits and to the men on the walls watching them. "There are only a few ways out of here and, if we go that way, they'll see us for sure." He catches a glimpse of her smile as, keeping low, she leads him up the stone steps.

"There's a secret way out of this ancient city…"

XXIX

After climbing the stairway of the ancient pyramid to reach the first platform, Jon and Rebecca check to see that all is clear. Jon catches his breath. "No one is here..."

"Good... Let's keep going."

Glistening with sweat, hearts pounding, they start to ascend the next set of steep stairs. Scrambling up on all fours, Jon looks back to scan the park, as several rounds of gunfire are exchanged below. He determines that none of the shooting is directed at them and breathes a sigh of relief. Reaching the top, Jon sees partial walls that were once a temple and, beyond it, a picturesque view of the ocean. Breathing heavily, Rebecca helps him up and then opens her arms to the amazing scenery. "Hey Jon... Not too bad, eh?"

"Stunning..."

Coba Libre

From behind one of the stone columns, a man steps out and points a machine gun at them. Jon stares at the man's outfit, trying to decide which criminal faction he belongs to. He looks to Rebecca, and she mirrors his confusion.

Speaking in a thick local accent, the mobster grumbles, "I figured Julio would be up to his old tricks."

Jon blurts out, *"Who's Julio?"*

Unamused, the mobster jabs his gun barrel at the pair. "Funny... I saw you both with him, so cut the shit."

The aim of the gun's muzzle settles on Jon, so he slowly raises his hands. "Oh, *that* Julio..."

"Do you have the book?"

Rebecca speaks up, "We left it where they instructed." The aim of the gun turns to her, and the man shakes his head. "Wrong answer."

Stepping forward to shield her, Jon lowers his arms to take off the backpack. "I have the book here."

She whispers, "If we give it to him, he'll kill us."

Wagging the gun barrel at Jon, he motions for the pack. "Open that bag and let me see."

Jon drops to a knee, opens the backpack and reaches in. He hesitates and then looks up. The mobster takes a step forward, leans over to peer inside the backpack and spots the valuable book stuffed between some of Jon's personal items. "Take it out..."

As Jon puts his fingers around the wrapped book, he feels something cold bump against the back of his hand. Reluctant, he looks up at Rebecca, and she gives him a nod. "Okay Jon, go ahead... Give it to him."

The mobster lowers his gun and reaches his hand out. "Listen to the smart Señorita."

Jon exhales and starts to remove his hand from the bag. Looking up at the mobster, he innocently asks, "You'll let us go when you have it?"

"Oh, yeah… Sure…

"Really?"

"Give it here…"

Jon jerks his hand from the bag and swings out with the Mayan ceremonial dagger. The mobster leaps to the side, and the obsidian blade slices across the hand holding the gun. Knuckles cut to the bone, the mobster clutches the bleeding wound and cries, "I will kill you for that!" Slashing once again, Jon catches the back of the man's wrist, and the machine gun drops to the ground.

Before the mobster can scoop it up, Jon reaches for it, grabbing the loose gun. He points it threateningly at the man and motions for him to step away. "Get back, or I'll shoot…" Suddenly, the ammo clip drops out and clatters to their feet. They both look down, then at each other. The mobster grins. "You need that part to make it work."

Behind them, Rebecca exclaims, "Jon! *Grab it…!!!*"

When he turns to look at her, the mobster takes the opportunity to snatch the ammunition clip from the ground. Pivoting back with the machine gun, Jon points it at the man. The mobster clutches the ammo clip in his hand and glares. "What are you gonna do now, *gringo*?"

Unsure, Jon looks past the mobster to the ocean. Without giving it much thought, he hurls the machine

Coba Libre

gun over the side. They hear it rattle down the stone wall and crash into the rocks at the bottom. Shocked, the man stands holding the ammo clip. He looks at where the machine gun went and then back to Jon. Tossing it aside, he puts up his bloody fists and steps forward. "Now, you will die the hard way…"

XXX

After slipping his arms back through the straps of his pack, Jon holds the Mayan dagger out threateningly. "Stay back!" The mobster smiles, stretches a little, and takes a few practice jabs with his fist. Seeing the blood streaking from the wounds, Jon gets sick to his stomach.

The mobster motions Jon closer and speaks brusquely. "Come over here niño, and I'll snap your neck quick."

Keeping the dagger held out in front, Jon backpedals. Nervously, he looks over his shoulder at Rebecca and asks, "What should we do?"

"I wouldn't have tossed the gun over the wall."

The sound of multiple gunshots from the fight below echoes in the distance. Jon turns around to face his opponent. The mobster lunges, and Jon, instinctively slashing out with the knife and jumps aside to dodge the blow. A piece of the man's shirt sleeve flaps open and everyone is quite surprised.

Despite the intimidating aggressiveness of the mobster, intense fear and survival instinct give Jon the courage to fight. He waves the dagger out in front of him defensively and warns, "I don't want to hurt you…"

The mobster inspects the slice on his shirt and then glares at Jon. "But, I *want* to hurt *you*…" He swings, missing, and then charges forward. Jon holds the knife out to block, but he is tumbled over and smashed to the floor. Grappling, the two roll across the rock surface, until they stop with the thug on top. With one hand restraining the wrist with the knife and the other wrapped around Jon's neck, the mobster growls, "You give me much trouble for a pequeño gringo…"

Rebecca runs up and gives a swift kick to the man's midsection. The solid whack barely gets the man's attention, and he turns his head to scowl at her. "Hold on, Señorita… You're next!" Beneath him, Jon squirms, using his free hand and all his strength in an attempt to push his attacker off. Firmly planted, the mobster squeezes Jon's neck tighter and pins the hand with the dagger to the stone floor.

Police sirens wailing in the distance get their attention. The mobster sits up to look around, easing his grip briefly. Suddenly, a slab of stone smashes into the side of his head and shards of rock rain down on Jon. Once again, the mobster turns to look at Rebecca with anger in his eyes and shakes his head. "I said your turn is coming!" Keeping one hand on Jon's neck, he uses his other to brush flecks of stone from the side of his face.

Coba Libre

Using the momentary distraction, Jon pushes the ceremonial dagger upward, stabbing into the man's abdomen. The man howls in agonizing pain and then glares at Jon.

The murderous rage on the man's face makes Jon panic, and he impulsively pulls the knife out. The uneven edges of the obsidian blade tear a jagged hole and increase the inflicted pain by opening the wound further. Jon gasps, "I'm *sorry…!*"

Now bearing down on Jon's neck with both hands, the mobster growls in anger. "I *kill* you…!!!"

Sensing that he is close to losing consciousness, Jon thrusts the ceremonial knife upward again and then pulls it out, hardly believing what he's doing. With eyes that display both pain and horror, the mobster releases his grip on Jon's neck and swats at the dagger. The bloody knife skitters across the stone floor, and Jon uses the brief respite to push off his attacker. Mustering almost the last of his energy, Jon arches his torso, just as Rebecca delivers a swift kick to the mobster's backside. The combined momentum pitches the man forward over Jon's shoulders and against a low stone wall overlooking the ocean. After rolling away, Jon climbs to a knee and gulps for air, as he watches the man struggle to stand while holding his blood-soaked abdomen.

Recognizing that they are still very much in jeopardy, Jon considers their options and glances at Rebecca. He touches his aching neck, takes a breath and charges ahead at the man. Surprised by Jon's audacity, the mobster side-steps the feeble attack and then accidentally slips on the blood-covered knife. Catching the mobster off-balance, Jon uses the opportunity to give him an extra shove. The man stumbles back against the low wall and, desperately grasping at empty air, he goes over the top and tumbles to the rocky shoreline below. Jon braces himself against the barrier and looks down.

When Jon turns around to look at Rebecca, she stares at him with a stunned expression. "Uh, Jon... *Wow...!*"

Still catching his breath, Jon takes a last look at the dead body and slides down the wall to sit next to the bloody knife. "I thought we were going to die."

"That was his plan."

The wail of police sirens steadily gets closer, and the popping of gunshots starts to dissipate in the park below. Slumped against the wall, Jon looks at the dagger beside him. His gaze travels to his backpack. "What do we do now?"

"Let's get out of here." She picks up his bag and smiles. "Don't forget your knife..." Rebecca waves him along, as she moves across the elevated platform to the other side.

"Yeah..." Grabbing the ceremonial blade by the handle, he tries to wipe some of the blood off against the stone floor. Looking up, just as Rebecca disappears around the corner of a broken column, he calls after her, "Hold on... *Wait for me!*"

XXXI

From the top platform of the pyramid, Jon looks down to see several gun-toting cartel members approaching. He also notices numerous police vehicles racing toward the park. Through the jungle canopy, beyond the ancient city's walls, the twinkling of their flashers makes the road light up like a holiday parade. Following Rebecca, Jon dashes around the corner of the stone structure and finds her unblocking another sealed passage. Looking to the exposed opening and the pile of discarded stones, he asks, "Does this one lead to a cenote, too?"

"No such luck…"

Jon looks back and moves to a better spot, where he can observe the group advancing from below. He turns back to her. "Uh, … There are quite a few men with guns climbing up here. Are we going to be able to hide inside?"

"Not exactly..." He looks confused, as she continues, "This will lead us to the sea wall."

"It's an escape passage?"

"More or less..."

Rebecca pulls another rock away, sizes up the small opening and squeezes inside. She disappears into the darkness and then pokes her head out to smile at him. "C'mon, Jon... What are you waiting for? Let's go!"

He sees her duck back into the dark hole and then looks down at the men clamoring up the steep steps. Dagger in hand, Jon leans down and peers into the partially open passage. "What do you mean, *more or less*?"

~*~

Jon follows Rebecca through the narrow tunnel until it opens to a large empty chamber. A rush of stale air surges past them to flow out the reopened entrance. The chamber's only illumination comes from the opening at the end of the passage, until Rebecca clicks on her flashlight. As she shines it around, Jon whispers, "I'm glad you carry one of those."

The bright ray of light briefly catches her sparkling eyes. "It's part of my job, and I do this sort of thing all the time."

"Getting chased by bad guys...?"

"No... Exploring Mayan ruins..."

Jon watches, as she points the beam of light in front of them to reveal the rest of the chamber. He asks, curiously, "Have you been in here before?"

"Once..."

"Where did you come out?"

Coba Libre

The beam flashes up to the low ceiling, and she replies, "The same way we came in…"

They move ahead, touching the narrowing walls, until they find two separate passageways before them. Jon looks back to the hint of daylight at the entrance, a good distance behind them, and observes silhouetted figures pass across it. He gulps and looks at Rebecca. "That might not be an option."

She points the flashlight at the choice of paths ahead. "Which way…? Corridor number-one or two…?"

Stumped, he looks at her in the hope that she's joking. "You know these things better than I do." He looks behind to the entrance. "I trust you."

She smiles at him sweetly and takes hold of his hand. "Okay… Let's try this one." The light clicks off, and she guides him forward through the darkness.

~*~

At the other end of the passageway, there is a trace of daylight shining in from the outside. Forward through the increasingly tight space, they crawl, single file, along the floor. Eventually, they turn a corner and look out to open sky, where the ocean meets the horizon. Moving up and squeezing in beside Rebecca at the break in the wall, Jon looks down at the waves crashing far below. He sighs, "That's a long way down. I guess we should have taken the other tunnel."

"Actually, the other one only leads to a catacomb."

"What?"

"It's a dead end."

Jon judges the distance to the waves crashing below. *"And, this one isn't…?"* Rebecca doesn't reply. After a moment, he nods his head understandingly. "So, this is the *only* way out of here?"

"Unfortunately…"

He looks down to the swelling waves that smash against the cliff wall below the pyramid. "If we jump, how deep is it?"

She pokes her head farther outside to judge the water. "If the tide is in, I should think it's deep enough."

Hearing muffled voices in the chamber behind them, they exchange a look of trepidation. Jon realizes that there is no time for hesitation and starts to take off his backpack. "Okay, I'll try to squeeze out there first."

"Oh, what a gentleman…"

He looks at her, sees that she's joking, then shimmies sideways through the opening to get past her. Once outside, he clings to the rocky face of the stone wall and looks up to the stacked mound of ruins above them. He tries to get a finger-hold in the seams between stones, but the rocks fit tightly.

Rebecca sticks her head out and watches him consider an attempt to ascend the wall. "I don't think we can climb up."

"I don't either." He stands on a narrow ledge and looks down at the water below which appears to be at an even greater distance because of the exposure.

The ocean breeze blows, and Rebecca sweeps her hair back and asks, "Are you okay?"

He shakes his head. "Not really… Come on out."

Coba Libre

Rebecca hands him his backpack and Jon slips his arms through the shoulder straps to hold the bag against his chest. She wriggles her way through the opening and clings to the stone wall beside him. When she looks at him, Jon timidly asks, "What's next...? I guess we jump?"

Perched on the ancient cliff wall as the wind blows, Rebecca moves over and gently puts her hand to Jon's cheek. She leans in and gives him a kiss. Despite the waves breaking below and the wall of tightly fitted stones stacked above them, the two connect as if nothing else mattered.

Finally, breaking from their passionate embrace, Rebecca looks out to the expansive view. "We'll be okay... Remember, take a breath, and jump off as far as you can."

To gather his courage, Jon inhales and then blows it out. Taking in her wind-blown beauty, he suggests, *"Ladies first...?"*

Rebecca grins. "It's been fun, Jon Springer!" She gives his hand a squeeze, releases it, crouches down and jumps.

Jon clutches his pack, takes a deep breath and pushes off from the wall. "Wait for *meeee!!!"*

XXXII

With a splash, Jon hits the water. He plunges deep, and the buoyancy of his backpack quickly brings him to the surface. First thing, he looks around for Rebecca. A wave pushes him toward the wall, washes over his head, and he tries to swim. His head bobs just above the swirling water and he calls out, "Rebecca… *Rebecca…?!?*"

A large wave lifts him up, carries him across the surf, and smashes him hard against the rocky face of the sea wall. The sudden blow knocks the wind from his chest, and Jon gasps for air while trying to spit out a mouthful of water. Swimming, he keeps his head above the churning waves and continues to search for Rebecca. Another wave crashes over him, and the swirling surge of water sweeps him out to sea.

~*~

Coba Libre

Floating in the ocean, clinging to the pack on his chest, Jon faintly hears a recognizable voice. Like an angel calling him, he hears, "*Jon... Jon...* Are you alive, Jon?"

Eyes fluttering open, Jon feels the saltwater burn them. He tries to focus in spite of the glare of sunlight reflecting from the surface. Slowly, the image of an inflatable raft takes shape. Leaning over the port side, a woman reaches out to him. Struggling to lift his head, Jon blinks and murmurs, "Rebecca... Rebecca...?"

Strong hands pull Jon into the raft, bend him over a knee and pump water from his lungs. Following a fit of coughing, Jon's vision clears enough for him to look around the raft and see Angie and Carlos' man, Jorge, staring back at him. Concerned, Angie puts her hand on Jon's arm to steady him. "Hey, Jon... It's lucky we found you before you drowned."

Coughing up another bit of seawater, Jon, in the bottom of the raft, sits up. He looks to Jorge and then to Angie. "How...?"

Comfortingly, she squeezes his arm. "How what?"

"Angie... How did you get here to find me?"

She gestures to the big pleasure yacht, owned by Carlos, not too far out to sea. Leaning close to Jon, she almost laughs. "With most people, when you hear police sirens and gunfire, they think to go the other way. We figured that just might be the place you would be."

Jon looks to the wet backpack tucked near his feet. Pulling it to his lap, he coughs again. "Thanks for the rescue. Did you find anyone else?"

Angie scans the water between them and the coastline. "No... just you." She turns to him. "Who is Rebecca?"

Jon considers the surging waves crashing against the sea wall below the ruins, and then lowers his gaze. "She's the friend that helped me get out of there."

"I'm sorry. You're the only one we found."

Laying back in the raft, Jon takes a breath and watches, as Jorge takes up the oars and starts to row them to the yacht. His head turns to Angie, and he looks at her questioningly. "You came here with Carlos?"

She gives him a telling expression and rolls her eyes. "Yeah, and that Cuban is treating it like it's our honeymoon." Jon can't help but grin, so Angie punches him in the shoulder. He feigns inflicted pain, holds his wet backpack and looks out over the rolling water toward the coastline. Up high, on the hill, the faint flicker of police lights flash beside the ancient ruins. With no sign of Rebecca, he heaves a disappointed sigh and silently mourns her loss.

~*~

In dry clothing, Jon steps out onto the deck of the yacht. Obviously borrowed from Carlos, the outfit makes him look like he is on vacation in the Caribbean. Wind sweeps through Jon's hair, as he stands at the railing. He watches the coastline of the Yucatan steadily pass by, as they travel northbound.

Carlos comes out of the galley with a drink in his hand. Jon turns, when he hears him approaching. The exceedingly well-dressed Cuban takes a sip from his cocktail and chuckles. "Well, well, well... If it isn't Mister

Coba Libre

Springer... You are worse for wear each time I come to rescue you."

With a nod, Jon looks down at his guayabera shirt. "Thanks for the loan of clothing."

Carlos sips from his drink, then lifts his glass as if making a toast. "Not a problem... My wardrobe is vast."

"Where are we headed?"

"Back to the Florida Keys, eventually."

"How long until we get there?"

Joining Jon at the port railing, Carlos breathes in the fresh ocean air. He turns to Jon and explains, "It is about a day and a half trip back to Key West, but first I need to take care of some business in Havana."

With a concerned look, Jon turns to meet his gaze. "Don't you think I've pushed my luck a bit with Cuba?"

The Cuban takes a drink and smiles his Cheshire grin. "Jon, you seem to be pushing your luck everywhere you go. Not to worry... Everything is arranged."

Behind them, Angie, scantily dressed in a bikini top and sarong, emerges from the galley with a can of beer in her hand. Both men turn and can't help but notice her athletic figure. Beaming with excitement, Carlos gives her a sweeping bow and reaches for her hand to kiss. "Ahh, our esteemed guest."

Unimpressed, Angie swats his outstretched hand away. "Cut the bullshit, Carlos." She opens the beer and takes a sip. "I told you to stop doing that thing."

Recovering quickly, Carlos winks at Jon and then smiles at Angie. "You, my dear are the model of decorum."

Taking a spot at the railing next to them, Angie looks Jon over and grins at his borrowed wardrobe. "How ya feelin'?"

"I'm still a bit off, but I'll be okay, I guess. Have you heard anything from Julio or Rollie?"

As if on cue, there is a throaty rumble in the distance, and they all turn their attention up toward the northern sky. The distinct outline of a flying boat comes into view and dips a wing in their direction. Jon instantly recognizes the familiar sight of Rollie's seaplane and sighs with relief.

Beside him, Angie takes another swallow from her beer and taps the can on the railing. "Speak of the devil…"

XXXIII

Carlos swirls the cubes of ice in his cocktail glass, as the seaplane flies past and circles back around for a water landing. "I would say Rollie is like a cat with nine lives… But, I think he has used up many more than that." Moving down the railing to press the button for the ship's intercom, Carlos speaks into the microphone. "The transportation for our guests has arrived. Please cut the engines, and bring Señor Springer's belongings up to the rear deck."

Everyone watches, as the seaplane approaches, touches down with a splash, and taxies up to the slow-moving yacht. Jon can see Rollie sitting behind the controls. He turns to Angie and asks, "Are you coming with us?"

She chugs the remainder of her beer, crunches the can, and tosses her empty in a bin meant for towels. She remarks, "If you think I'm staying here on the *Cuban Love Boat* for another minute, you're mistaken."

Carlos overhears her and smiles his Cheshire grin. "Aww, Sweetie… I could show you a good time in Havana."

She shakes her head and saunters off to the galley. "Yeah, I bet… I'll go get my bag."

While watching her go, the Cuban whistles under his breath. He moves over next to Jon again and comments, "Ah, Señor Springer, I must thank you for getting into much trouble, so Angie feels she has to come rescue you. It seems, the more danger you get into, the more I get to see her."

Jon looks at Carlos sheepishly. "The recent events were *not* of my doing."

"Nevertheless…" Carlos turns, as Jorge appears at the doorway to the galley. He is holding Jon's soaking-wet backpack and a small bundle in a trash sack. "Unfortunately, we did not have time to launder and dry your things."

Jon glances down at his high-priced borrowed outfit. "Okay if I return your wardrobe in Key West…?"

"Of course."

Reaching out, Jon goes over to retrieve his belongings. With a sodden thud, Jorge drops everything to the deck. Watching the big gorilla of a man turn to the stairway leading to the lower deck, Jon mutters, "Thanks…"

~*~

The nose-hatch opens on the seaplane and Rollie pops up with a tether line in hand. "Ahoy, there!" He tosses the coil of rope to Jorge and looks to see Jon and Carlos descending the rear deck stairway. "Hey, Jon...! Ready to get back home?"

"Yeah, I've had enough vacation for a while."

Rollie shrugs with embarrassment. "Sorry about that..."

Stepping up to the railing, Jon hands his backpack and bag of wet clothes over to Rollie. "Have you heard from Julio?"

Rollie gives a quick nod, "Let's get clear of here first, and I'll fill you in on the details." He looks past Jon to see Angie coming with her duffle bag, and grins when he sees her outfit. She sports a *Key West Air Charters* shirt loosely buttoned over her bikini top. "Hey, Jon... It looks like you're out of a job on the return flight." Smiling, the pilot takes Angie's bag and ducks down, as Jon helps her step over to the nose-hatch.

Carlos pretends to wipe a tear from his eye and waves to her with his handkerchief. "Goodbye for now, my lovely... I'll see you again soon at the *Conch Republic Tavern*!

With a disgusted look, Angie turns and waves him off. "See ya later. Thanks for your help."

"Anytime, my dear... Your chariot awaits!

Before stepping over to the seaplane, Jon turns to Carlos. "Thanks again, Carlos... I owe you."

"Señor Springer, I look forward to coming to your aid during your next adventure."

Jon gets a sensation of dread, as he catches Jorge glaring at him from the aft sundeck. Then, as Rollie slips behind the controls, Jon steps over to the flying boat and ducks into the nose of the seaplane.

Untethered from the pleasure yacht, the seaplane drifts away as the nose-hatch is pulled closed. The radial engines, perched high on each wing, pop and then rumble to life. Propellers whirling, the seaplane turns out to open water, slowly accelerating through the rolling waves.

On the deck with Jorge, Carlos stands watching the departure. The seaplane races across the water, lifts into the sky and, with a mist of spray trailing from the hull, banks away to the east. Carlos lifts a hand to curtly wave farewell. "So long… Until next time, my friends."

~*~

Up front, seated in the copilot chair, Jon adjusts his headphones and speaks through the airplane's intercom. "Rollie, thanks again for coming to get me."

With a nod, the pilot replies, "I just have to say again how sorry I am that you got mixed up with all that."

Jon lowers his gaze to his lap for a moment, then looks up and out the window. He stares into the distance while reflecting on recent events. "I'm so sorry about Rebecca…"

Rollie adjusts his sunglasses and looks over at Jon. "Why…? She's fine."

Perked up, Jon smiles in disbelief. *"Really?"*

"None too happy with Julio, of course… But, she's her same beautiful self, last I saw her before taking off to get you." The pilot takes a folded card from his shirt pocket and hands it over to Jon. "She gave me this to give to you."

Jon takes the folded paper but is hesitant to open it. "What will happen to Julio?"

"He'll be okay. He gets mixed up with this sort of stuff all the time. The thing is, he's got dirt on everyone from the American border all the way down into Central America." Rollie reaches up to adjust the two overhead throttle levers. "I'm one of the few that he doesn't pull the strings on, or he'd have me doing charter flights for his unscrupulous operations. If he told you that he was in real danger, it was because he was playing you to get the angle on something else."

Jon thinks about his interactions with Julio and then on the strong words of caution from Ace. "I guess I was warned." He looks the pilot over. "How are you after all this?"

Rollie shrugs. "They roughed me up a bit, but nothing more than a late-night boxing match would do. They wanted to use my airplane to recover that contraband off the coast." Looking over his sunglasses, he tilts his head at Jon and smirks. "That damned Julio beat them to it though, and then he sold almost everything they wanted to recover back to them! Heck, I expect he made out like a bandit."

"What about the Mayan treasure?"

Rollie gives Jon a strange look and then turns ahead. "Treasure...? I don't know about any treasure."

Peering over his shoulder to the cargo area, Jon sees his empty backpack and Angie spreading out his wet belongings. He looks back to Rollie and then adjusts the headset microphone, "Uh… Julio said they were holding you to trade for a book with directions to an ancient Mayan treasure."

The pilot gives Jon a telling glance and has to keep himself from laughing. "Really…? Ancient Mayan treasure… Sounds like something he might say."

Getting the sinking sensation that he's been used as a pawn, Jon slips the unopened letter from Rebecca into his pants pocket and sits back in the copilot seat. He tries not to dwell on his feelings from recent events. Looking out at the expansive blue ocean, he settles into the droning sound of the dual overhead engines.

XXXIV

The Key West Air Charters pickup truck rolls up in front of the Conch Republic Tavern. The passenger-side door opens, and Jon exits to let Angie slide out from the middle. She gives Jon a big hug and then grabs her few belongings from the truck bed. "You coming in later to have a drink?"

The truck's rusty door hinge creaks, as he leans on it. "Yeah, just want to drop my stuff off and freshen up a bit first."

She starts to go, then turns back and raises an eyebrow. "For an aspiring writer without any ideas, you sure live an interesting life, Jon Springer."

Grateful, Jon steps to Angie and gives her another hug. "Thanks for the rescue. Once again…"

"That's what friends are for." She watches him get back into the truck, and then waves to them as they drive off. Turning to face the tavern, she looks up at the carved sign over the door and murmurs to herself. "There is something about this island that feeds the adventurous soul…"

~*~

Rollie steers the old truck down the streets of Key West. He turns the corner, heading toward Jon's place, and spots Casey Kettles on the sidewalk. He gives a honk and takes his foot off the gas pedal. As they roll past the gangly teenager, Casey bends down, looks into the truck cab and sees Jon.

He lowers his yellow sunglasses to get a better look and then, with a mischievous smile, pushes them up again. Catching the odd expression, Jon looks to Rollie as he shifts gears. "What was that look about?"

Rollie drives on, and grumbles, "Probably nothing… That's just how the kid is."

"Did you want to talk with him?"

"Nope… Just letting him know I'm watching."

They pull up and stop at the side entrance nearest to the estate's garage apartment. Jon gets out and leans down to look at Rollie through the rolled-down, passenger-side window. "Thanks, Rollie." He reaches into the truck bed, grabs his gear and peeks back into the cab. "It was… *interesting.*"

The pilot swats the gear shifter into neutral and shrugs. "At Key West Air Charters, we aim to please." Jon laughs, thumps the truck roof with his hand and steps to the curb. Giving a wave, Jon watches as the truck shifts into low gear and then drives off. Feeling a distinct lack of danger and sudden drain of adrenaline, he looks around at the empty street. Finally, he turns on a heel and steps through the garden gate.

~*~

Carrying his backpack on his shoulder and the trash bag full of damp clothes at his side, Jon enters the apartment and clicks on the floor lamp nearest to the door. In a somber mood, he drops the trash bag on the tile floor, then sets the backpack on the coffee table and takes a deep breath. Before he can sit, the phone rings.

Jon grabs the phone from the cradle and answers, "Hello…?"

A professional-sounding voice on the line replies, "Hello, Jon Springer. I have C. Moselly for you."

Jon looks around the room for a clock, and then down at his wristwatch. "Uh, sure…" He waits a moment, until his agent gets on the call.

"Hey there, Johnny-boy!"

"Hey, Moselly…"

"I've been trying to find you for days."

Carrying the telephone base, trailing the cord along, Jon moves over to the couch. "Did you read the manuscript?"

"Yeah, that's what I wanted to talk to you about…"

Jon sits down and looks at the backpack slumped in the middle of the coffee table. "Well…?"

"Are you playing a joke on me?"

"No… What…? You didn't like it?"

There is a prolonged silence, until an office chair shifts with a squeak, and then creaks as it tilts back. Coughing, Moselly clears his throat and continues with the conversation. "It's fine, mostly, but... How do I say this, uh, well... *nicely?*" The agent leans closer to the speakerphone. "It's *boring*... Where's the action, adventure, tropical locations, and the lust in the dust with beautiful maidens?!?"

"It doesn't have any of that."

"Yeah, I noticed!!!"

Disappointed, Jon scoots down and lays his head back. "You don't want to publish it?"

"It's just not a J. T. Springs novel. Your loyal fans would burn it, like they were a bunch of angry Nazis on parade."

"Thanks, Moselly..."

"They'd run you out of town tarred and feathered!"

"Don't sugar-coat it for me."

The agent spins in his chair. Then, it creaks, as he leans back to put his feet up on the desk. "Listen, pal. We've made a lot of money together. How about this... We publish this turd, uh, I mean turkey... No, no, no, I mean *tasteful* novel, under a Jonathan Springer pen name, and then you crank me out another J. T. Springs novel that I can sell the hell out of."

Mildly upset, but not really surprised, Jon nods his consent, as he reaches forward to unbuckle his backpack. "Sure... Fine... I think I have something in mind." He opens the pack, and a mess of wet toiletries tumble out. He pushes them to the floor and wipes the dampness from the table's surface. Moving the bag, the book, still wrapped in plastic, slides out.

Eric H. Heisner

On the other end of the line, Moselly spins his creaky leather chair around and leans in toward his speakerphone. "Great! Glad to hear it! When do I get some of those pages? Where is it set, and what is the storyline?"

Jon picks up the plastic-wrapped book and inspects it. Reaching into the damp backpack, he takes out the Mayan ceremonial knife and slices through the waterproof covering. Cradling the phone receiver between his neck and shoulder, concentrated on unwrapping the book, Jon answers candidly. "I was thinking it could take place in Quintana Roo, Mexico. Maybe around the ancient city of Coba…"

Excited, Moselly chimes in, "Great!!! I can see it now: *Coba Libre,* with Mexican chicas spinning in flower skirts and shirtless dudes in sombreros… Maybe some small donkeys… I'll start planning the premiere!"

Jon interrupts, "The drink is actually *Cuba Libre*."

Unfazed, Moselly retorts, "Not if you're in Mexico!" Continuing to ramble on, he spouts off about bullfights, mariachis, and tequila.

Pulling away the plastic covering to reveal a tome that looks to be a hundred years old, he handles the book delicately. After inspecting the writing on the spine, he looks to the ceremonial dagger in his other hand and interrupts Moselly. "Maybe something to do with the Mayans…"

"Huh…? Mayans…? You mean those short people in the Wizard of Oz???"

Turning the brittle pages of the book, Jon sees lines of notes along the margins with several hand-drawn sketches. "Roads paved with gold, maybe... Legends of maps through the jungle to ancient treasure..."

"Now you're talking!!! Send me the pages, as soon as you got 'em. I got another call coming in, but get on it."

"Bye, Moselly..."

The call disconnects. Jon hangs up the telephone. He puts the antique book and the Mayan dagger on the table, before taking the folded note from Rebecca out of his pocket. He looks outside, through the palm trees, to the tropical sunset, as the evening glow begins to fade. Leaning over to the standing lamp next to the couch, Jon clicks it on and sits back to open the letter and read.

The End...

If you enjoyed **Conch Republic vol. III**,
read other stories by
Eric H. Heisner

www.leandogproductions.com

T. H. Elkman

Tale of a Wandering Cowboy

A Western novel by

Eric H. Heisner

www.leandogproductions.com

WEST TO BRAVO

A Western Novel

By Eric H. Heisner

WWW.LEANDOGPRODUCTIONS.COM

Wings of the Pirate

A high-flying Adventure Novel

By Eric H. Heisner

Limited time pre-order at:

www.inkshares.com

Illustrations by

Al P. Bringas

www.leandogproductions.com

Eric H. Heisner is an award-winning writer, actor and filmmaker. He is the author of several Western and Adventure novels: *West to Bravo, T. H. Elkman, Africa Tusk, the Conch Republic series,* and *Short Western Tales: Friend of the Devil.* He can be contacted at his website: <u>www.leandogproductions.com</u>

Emily Jean Mitchell is an artist, teacher, and mother who enjoys spending time in the garden and outdoor playtime with her husband, children and dog in Austin, Texas.

www.mlemitchellart.com

Made in United States
North Haven, CT
30 August 2023

40960438R00125